ETERNALLY YOURS

ETERNALLY YOURS

DRUID DUO BOOK TWO

CARLY SPADE

ETERNALLY YOURS

DRUID DUO BOOK TWO

Copyright © 2025 by Carly Spade

WWW.CARLYSPADE.COM

Published in the United States by World Tree Publishing, LLC

Cover by Story Wrappers

WWW.STORYWRAPPERS.COM

Interior Formatting by We Got You Covered Book Design

WWW.WEGOTYOUCOVEREDBOOKDESIGN.COM

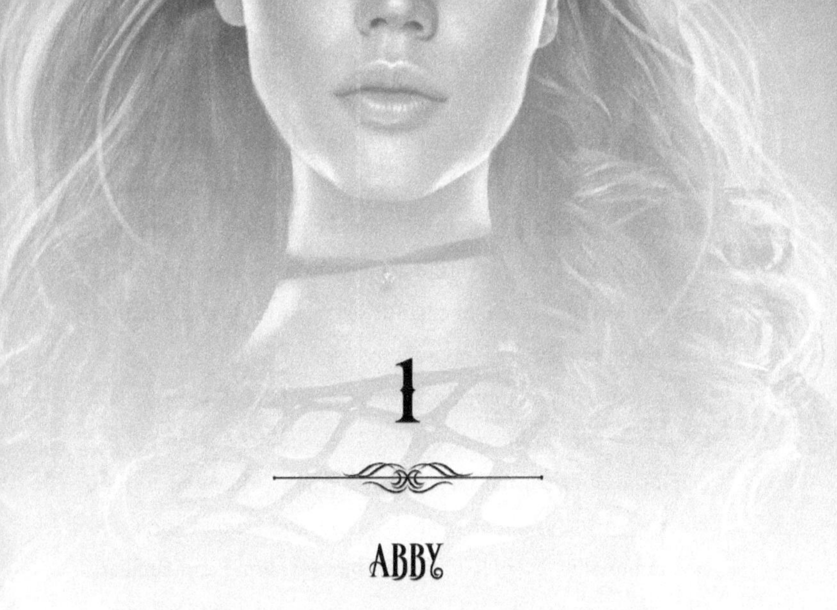

1

ABBY

EIGHT WEEKS AND TWO DAYS. Two. Whole. Months. And my stubborn ass Druid was still nowhere to be seen, not to mention the fact that I hadn't heard from him in weeks. *Weeks.* What was a newly reborn Druid supposed to think? Had he abandoned me? Died? Been kidnapped? Had a complete and utter change of heart, deciding I was too much to handle?

We were forced to part ways the *day* after he'd saved my life. Erimon gave me a part of his soul and his power to keep me alive. He'd bound himself to me in the only way a Druid could—transference. It all made the Bandruí side of me wake up. And with all of it also came a connected tattoo—my sleeve on the right, his on the left, and it allowed us to communicate beyond the nature whispering we'd done previously. I never imagined it could get any stronger.

Explaining the inexplicable and elaborate ink I'd gotten during my vacation to the zoo I worked for when I returned was another matter entirely. I avoided the conversation for a couple of weeks by always wearing long sleeves. But one day, while changing to get into the water with my favorite sea otter, Bruno, my boss caught sight of it, and I could only think to tell her that Ireland is a magical place of fairy tales and alcohol—lots and lots of alcohol. She hadn't seemed to approve, I didn't blame her, but she let it go nonetheless.

My job. I'd undoubtedly have to quit once I knew what Erimon needed from me, when I knew how we intended to defeat the Dullahan and keep me alive. When we knew where the Elder was so he could eternally bond me and Erimon and gain my immortality. Every last bit of it sounded absurd and familiar all in the same breath, and it was enough to make my head spin.

And poor Finn, the immortal giant charged as my mythical bodyguard, must be going stir crazy by now being cooped up in my cubicle-sized New York apartment. When he lay on the cot of over a dozen blankets I'd procured for him in my living room, we wouldn't be able to *move* if there'd been one more of him. Finn MacCoul, the hunter warrior who has slain creatures, demons, and tyrants, reduced to a Druid babysitter.

The absolute worst part was Erimon announcing that I would have one of his powers, but neither of us knew what it would be or when it would manifest. Every waking moment Erimon wasn't around me, I feared I'd miraculously launch pieces of the road into some poor pedestrian's chest cavity or skewer someone with iron pulled from a street sign. I'd seen Erimon use his powers countless times, and being in New York City with so many people to harm and not knowing how to control it *terrified* me.

I'd only seen Phoebe and Patrick, the leprechaun newlyweds,

a handful of times, given Patrick wanted to meet Phoebe's family and she needed to wrap up her life to go live a new mystical one. Which would also be me very soon—I hoped.

I lay half awake and groggy in bed, lazily twirling the Claddagh ring on my right hand, running my thumb over its grooved designs. A ring that started as a deal from a Druid for protection against the Dullahan in exchange for a kiss that turned into a symbol of our bond. Memories of our first days together—the jabs, the mystery, the chaos—brought a smile to my lips. The rising sun peeked through the blinds, its warmth pooling against my cheek.

I nuzzled into my soft emerald green blanket, comfortable and snuggled. That is, until Finn's booming voice roared, "Abby!"

Sitting up with a gasp and flying my eyes open, I stared at him in panic. "What is it?"

My sunflower curtains were on the floor, Finn had been stomping, and smoke still billowed from them.

"You caught your bleedin' curtains on fire, and are about to do it again." Finn's pale eyes widened, and his giant finger pointed at my hand.

When my gaze dropped, I let out a bubbled shriek at the sight of a fireball floating in my palm. "Oh my—take it away," I shrilled, shoving my hand toward Finn and accidentally launching more fire.

It landed on the coffee table, igniting a pile of magazines, and Finn scooped them up, tossing all fiery contents into the trash bin before using his boot to snuff the flames.

"I—" I couldn't help myself and went into a complete panic. Scrambling from the bed, I fanned my palms at Finn, attempting to apologize, and hurled fire *directly* at him instead.

It ignited a braid in Finn's blonde beard. He used two fingers to squelch it, leaving it half as long as it used to be, the ends singed. Growling, he snapped his steely gaze at me. "*Close* your hands, Abby."

Doing as he commanded and whimpering, trying to ignore the faint scents of burnt hair floating around us, I balled my hands into fists and clutched them under my chin. "I'm so sorry. I don't know how to control it."

Finn, who usually remained so positive and assured, sighed, shook his head, and dragged a hand down his chest-length beard. "Where in the seven hells is Erimon?"

My nose stung with threatening tears, and I gulped them back. "I'm sorry you have to deal with this, Finn. To deal with—me."

Finn's face fell, his expression softening before he crossed the room in one stride and hugged me. My face pressed against his tunic-covered stomach, and I began to weep. "No, no. There, there. I didn't mean it like that, girl. I'm just angry at him for takin' so long when *you* need him. Especially now. This isn't something I can protect you from."

"Trust me—" I started, my voice muffling from my nose still shoved against Finn. Lifting my chin, I rested it on his abdomen and sniffled. "—I feel *quite* the same way."

Abby, can ye hear me?

Erimon's voice trickled over my brain like static velvet, and I stilled, the Celtic tattoo on my arm sending rippling sensations through my skin.

"The nerve he has," I whispered through gritted teeth and rubbed the ink, attempting to make the sensation stop. It didn't.

Finn's massive hands gripped my shoulders, coaxing me back. "Who are you talkin' about?"

"Erimon," I snarled.

Abby, where are you?

The tattoo pulsed red.

Letting out a frustrated shriek, making sure to keep my hands in fists, I shrugged off Finn's touch and stomped to the kitchen. "He doesn't bother reaching out all this time, and now, when it's convenient for him he gets to be the one to be worried about *me*? Oh, no. Nope. I'm going to *ignore* him."

Finn approached with cautious steps, uncomfortably rubbing his neck before leaning on the opening of my quaint breakfast nook counter. "I've got to say I'm a tad confused. How do you know he's worried about you at this precise moment? I mean, clearly, he's worried about you, but—"

While Finn talked, I rummaged through several drawers, using only my knuckles to pull on the handles. "We can talk to each other." When Finn's bushy brows rose, still perplexed, I sighed and flopped a pair of oven mittens in front of him. "Through our minds. It's part of the bond or something."

Finn drummed his fingers on the fake marble. "Ah. Alright. Just something I figured would've been brought up sooner than now."

Had we not said anything? Surely at some point?

"We never told you all?"

Finn shook his head, the gold loops braided within his beard clinking together. "No. I'd certainly remember."

"Apologies and all that." I re-emphasized the mittens by nudging them toward him with a knuckle. "Help me put these on, please."

Frowning, Finn picked one up between two fingers like a wet sock and scrunched his nose. "You expect these puny things made of fabric to stop your fire powers?"

"They stop mortals from burning their hands on things that would otherwise scorch our skin. I figured—"

I was grasping at straws, and I knew that, but I also needed the use of my hands. It was worth a shot.

Finn continued to hold the mitten like a dirty diaper and arched a brow.

"Just help me put them on, please." Holding my fists up, I waited for him to relent and finally open each end. I didn't unclench my hand until the exact moment I could slip them on.

We both flinched, waiting for my kitchen table to suddenly become kindling, but, much to my chagrin, nothing happened.

Satisfied, I nodded. "Alright. Temporary fix."

Finn leaned on an elbow. "Are you really going to ignore him?"

Adjusting my mittens, I casually propped a hip on the counter and lifted my chin. "Yes."

"Isn't that a wee bit counterproductive, Abby?" Finn held back a smile almost entirely hidden by the bushy mustache and beard, but his dimples gave it away.

"Nope. Because I figure it'll get him here that much faster."

Finn held his head low before throwing it back with a chuckle. "You already know him so damn well. I applaud ye."

Strangely, I didn't feel like I knew him that well at all. We'd had our moments and various conversations. We shared a bond, soul, power, and intimate time together. I owed him my life—twice. But we still never had a chance just to *be* if such a thing was even possible for Druids.

"And now we just need to busy ourselves until he shows up," I said, raising my thumbnail to chew on it and sputtering when I received a mouthful of oven mitten instead.

Finn combed his beard, his gaze focused on the floor in thought. "We could play cards?"

Smirking, I held my mittens up.

"Right." Finn covered his mouth with a hand. "You'd probably wind up lighting them on fire anyway," he mumbled.

"Hey," I yelled.

Finn's massive shoulders shrugged. "What? It's true." He frowned and then brightened, snapping his fingers. "We could watch *Darby O'Gill*."

Rolling my eyes, I pinched the bridge of my nose. "We've watched it three times already, Finn."

His pout returned. "Well, it's a delightful motion picture show."

"How about we sit on the couch, drink some iced tea, and you tell me more stories about the Fianna warriors?"

That would distract him.

Finn's face lit up, he turned on his heel, and headed for the sofa.

"Would you mind pouring the drinks?" I waved a mitten at him.

"Right. Of course." Finn smiled and ducked into the kitchen, carefully opening the fridge so as not to yank the door from its hinges.

With tea in hand, we sat on the couch, and Finn regaled me with ancient stories I once believed to be nothing but myth. Gradually, his words faded into white noise, replaced by innumerable thoughts and memories of Erimon. I wasn't sure how I'd react when seeing him after all this time. Angry? Elated? Relieved? Probably all at once. But one thing I knew, I wasn't going to go easy on him. At least not right away. Yes. I'd make him *sweat* a little.

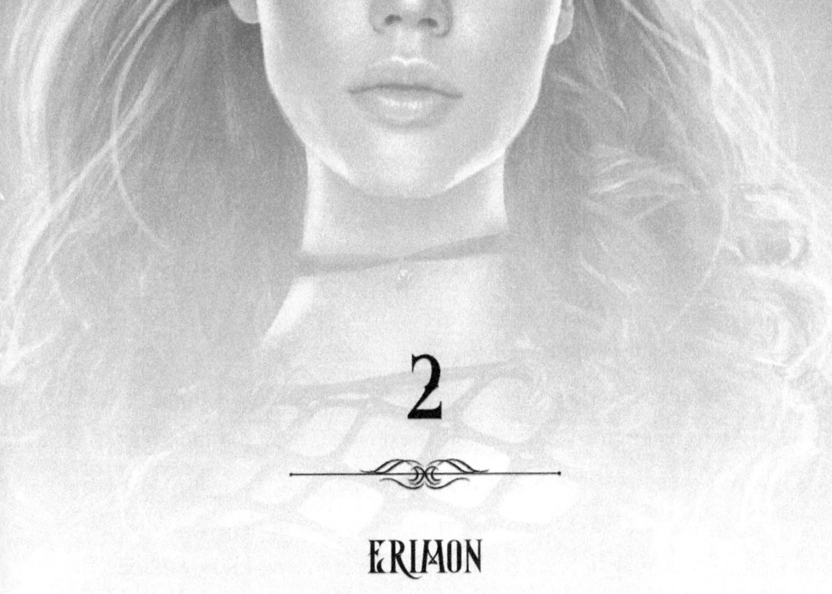

2

ERIMON

I DUCKED BEHIND A LOG, pressing my back against its bark, and blocked falling debris with my arms. Mave soon followed, kneeling beside me with her sword poised. The warrior queen goddess of Connacht was still as battle-hardened and fearless as when we fought the Dullahan together. She'd had no more reason to be loyal to me, given I'd told her she'd paid her debt fighting in her army to lay claim to Connacht, yet she remained, and I couldn't imagine defeating the death god without her.

"She's gonna murder you. You know that, right?" Mave raised a single, auburn eyebrow.

The 'she' Mave referred to being Abby, of course. When we last parted, I convinced her to go back home so we could wrap up loose ends here in Ireland, sending Finn to watch over her in my absence. I originally intended it as a means for her own safety away from the Dullahan, who still had her soul marked, but that was almost two months ago as of tomorrow. We'd made it to the barrier, the invisible wall that separates Earth from the Otherworld. We were even ready to battle all trials and tribulations to break past the Ninth Wave to make it into the Otherworld, but the Fomori—ferocious sea creatures—destroyed those plans.

The sun illuminated my palm, and a fireball sprung to life. After staring Mave down with a steely glare, I stood up long enough to hurl several streams of fire at the hundreds of demons surrounding us. One of the demons launched a fireball back towards me, and I ducked behind the log.

"She may be a tad miffed, but it's not like we knew we'd be contendin' with sluagh or the Fomori, for that matter, who, by the way, is still a problem, or have you forgotten?" The sluagh were demons conjured from dead mortal sinners—the Dullahan's newest henchmen. Not only did we have to worry about goblins, but we now have to worry about demons as well. It was grand.

Mave snickered. "For bein' a ladies' man, you sure don't know a thing about them, do ye?"

Mave could invoke fear in the hearts of any man who dared challenge her. I tried it once, and I'm still cleaning shite out of my trousers. She was the living embodiment of a feisty redhead with the skills to back it up.

Talk about your low blows. "I think I know them just fine. Is this really the time to talk about this?" I conjured another fireball and threw it over the log.

"*I'd* be livid. All that time waitin' to see if you'd even be coming back. Just *wrong*." She shook her head but bit back a smile.

I plucked a piece of bark from the log, rubbing it between

my fingers, looking anywhere but at her. "In my defense, I never specified a time frame."

Mave guffawed. "You're an eejit."

Gritting my teeth, I threw another bout of fire, taking out my increasing annoyance on the nearest demons. I plopped back to the ground with a huff. "Look, she has the ring. She can contact me any time her pretty 'lil heart desires. It's not my fault she hasn't in a couple weeks."

Mave smacked the back of my skull. "The silent treatment is universal lady code for—I'm pissed at ye, and I want you to contact *me*." And now, she patted my head like a dog.

I batted her hand away with a scowl. Mave was bordering on making complete sense, and it'd be a cold day in dubnos before I told her that. Once we were out of this mess, I'd check on Abby to ensure was alright, *not* because Mave suggested it. I stood, ready to throw another fireball but frowned, realizing my hand was empty. That's *odd*.

Mave stood, pushing me out of the way, and sliced her sword through an approaching sluagh. I continued to stare down at my palm, beside myself. My gaze didn't budge, even when Mave dragged me behind the safety of the log.

"Why were you standin' there like a daft mule?" Mave's voice screeched in my ear. "Havin' troubles *performing*, Erimon?" Her lips curled into a sly grin.

I scoffed, balling my hand into a fist, and clenched my jaw. "I've *never* had performance—complications."

Mave shrugged, still biting back that godsforsaken grin.

My fire power was on the fritz. No matter. The ground began to shake, and I opened my hands, spreading my fingers wide.

Mave's gaze moved to the dirt, hundreds of rocks escaping from it. Once they were all suspended in mid-air, I clenched my jaw, stood, and swung my arms forward. The rocks flew forward with the speed of bullets, plowing through the nearest enemy.

"Where the hell is, Cu, anyway?" Mave asked.

Cu Chulainn, or 'Hound,' was capable of a 'warp-spasm' where he'd morph himself into a hulking, distorted monster that became nearly indestructible. The last time we'd seen him, he was spasming through dozens of sluagh and went missing in action.

"That coward probably ran off," Mave continued before hoisting herself over the log, balancing on her hand. She swung her leg in a sweep, kicking one of them in the face, followed by her blade plunging into their gut.

"During his spasm? Oh, yes. I'm sure he stopped for afternoon tea," I countered.

Mave glared at me with such venom it may have made my knees shake was I a mortal.

Rolling my eyes, I added, "He took a lap. He's headed back around this way. Come on. I've grown bored of this. Time to wrap it up." I leaped over the log, smiling defyingly at the sluagh.

Mave walked to my side, sword at the ready. She launched into the demons that ran forward in droves. I shot one hand out to the side, splintering wood from nearby trees and pulled them toward me, slicing through enemies on the way. Dropping to one knee, I pressed my fingertips to the ground, summoning iron ore from beneath the surface to form a sword blade. I melded the metal to the wooden handle and swung it into several bodies.

Cu charged forward, his gaunt slow, but he could take out

seven or more beings with every swing of his enormous limbs. He ran past us, growling a battle cry. Apparently, he was going on *another* lap.

Mave put all her effort into swinging her sword, dodging, sliding and damn near back flipping her way through the demons, but at one point she began to get overrun. They started to dogpile over her, and I threw my hands forward. A gust of wind sent them all flying off her and into the tree branches. I threw my hand skyward, a slab of rock launching from the ground, giving her a blockade to fight with. She glanced at me, puffing a rogue strand of red hair from her face, and nodded a silent thank you.

"Together, Mave," I raised my sword into the air, while Mave followed suit. With perfect timing, Cu came back around and followed at our rear as we all began to charge forward, thunderous shouts echoing from our lungs.

The sluagh vanished, leaving us standing in the middle of a deserted clearing, swords held above our heads and our deafening cries echoing off the trees. We glanced around, lowering our blades, and Cu plowed into us. I stumbled forward, jabbing the tip of my sword into the ground to keep from falling. Realizing there was no one left to pummel, Cu grunted and turned around to look at us, chest heaving.

The faint sound of hands clapping started nearby, causing us to raise our weapons again and move into a defensive position.

"I must say, it all makes sense now. When the Dullahan approached me with such a proposition, I was astonished that he felt *threatened.*" He stepped out from the shadows of the trees, hands clasped behind him. He had three eyes formed in a triangle, the one at its point covered by a round metal plate and white hair running down the entire length of his back. The armor he wore was spiky, gnarled, and as black as his soul if he had one.

Cu morphed back into his human form, his lips parting. "Balor?"

It couldn't possibly be…

"Grandson. I was disappointed to hear of your involvement. I would hate to have to kill you over some petty mortal," Balor said.

My blood boiled at his words, and I stepped forward, but Mave's hand gripped my shoulder, coaxing me back.

"You're supposed to be dead," Cu said, pointing a finger into Balor's face.

"Oh, I was. Tell me, is my grandson Lug still living? I'd love to give him accolades for being so clever with that slingshot." Balor chuckled, his hands resting on the armor covering his abdomen.

"How are you alive?" Mave asked, her hands twisting over the handle of her sword.

"As you all know, before my unfortunate demise, I was the God of Death. The Dullahan served as a warning, a keeper of sorts for the souls destined to depart this world. After I died, he became both taker and keeper of the dead. He is a powerful creature, but realized that he'd be far *more* powerful if alleviated of the latter burden." A sinister grin played across his lips like a serpent.

My muscles tensed, fury building. Balor's return would only make our journey to the Otherworld more difficult. He was once the ruler of the Fomori and would now be their King again. With him and the Dullahan joining forces, we would need every abled ethereal being we could get our hands on if we had any hope of defeating them.

"Allow us to do you a favor and return you to your restin' place," Mave said, taking a few steps forward.

Balor half-smiled, dipping his chin before lifting it defiantly. "The Dullahan seeks but one human. Surely, her life isn't worth the lives of the hundreds that could be lost during the struggle?"

I no longer desired to hear the venom spewing from his mouth, so I hurled my sword towards Balor's head. He turned his face towards the approaching blade, waved a hand in the air, and the sword disintegrated into particles, floating into the wind. We all stood rigid, unable to hide our shock.

"You must be the Druid. The one supposedly bonded to the chosen? You'll be especially interesting to deal with." He grinned and rolled his shoulders, pieces of his white hair falling over his chest.

I stormed forward until Balor and I were nose to nose. "You won't touch one hair on her head." The ground began to rumble underneath my feet.

Balor's head tilted down, his stance widening as the rumbling intensified. Rock spikes shot through the ground from underneath Balor, launching him into the sky. My hands twitched, continuing to conjure the largest chunks of rock I could find beneath the surface of the ground. Balor fell to the dirt in a heap, his armor creaking, dust flying. I closed my hands into fists, my breathing becoming subdued snarls. It couldn't have been that easy.

Balor let loose a maniacal laugh, lifting his head and pushing himself to his feet. "You've got spirit, Druid. I'll certainly give you that." He tossed his long hair behind him, sputtering bits of grass that collected on his lips. "Just know this. Between the Dullahan and myself, we have goblins and sluagh at our disposal. And now that I've returned, I fully intend to take control back of the Fomori. You can forget about making it the Otherworld, and you can forget about saving dear, sweet Abigail. The God of Death *always* gets his way." He disappeared into a cloud of black smoke.

I let out a monstrous roar. "Why her of all humans? *Why?*"

"Have you ever stopped to wonder if this is not all part of a plan?" Mave said, letting the sword fall limp at her side.

"Fate? You're talking about *fate*, right now?" I wrung my hands together before dragging them over my beard in frustration.

"It's all too coincidental. Abby is a Bandruí now—a *Druid*. Perhaps hidin' her is the exact opposite of what we should be doing." Mave shrugged, sheathing her sword at her back.

When I'd performed the transference, giving Abby a part of my soul to save her life, it also gave her part of my Druidic power. Having never performed the ritual, I wasn't sure how much magic she would receive, nor what it would be. She *was* a Druid now. She became a part of me. She'd always been capable of handling herself, but now, with this power, she could help take on Balor and the Dullahan with brute force. No. It'd put her in even greater danger. I almost lost her once, I wasn't going to let it happen again.

I shook my head vigorously. "Absolutely not. Power or no

power, she's already in enough danger just being in their crosshairs. I won't take that risk."

Mave's eyebrows shot skyward. "Oh? And you're making her decisions for her now?"

Abby was headstrong, confident, and the least selfish person I knew. It was one of the many reasons I felt so drawn to her the first time in that pub. She'd fight tooth and nail if I asked her to stay back while the rest of us fought *for* her.

"No. But she'd agree with me and stay in America with Phoebe while we took care of it. Obviously." I sniffed, rubbing a knuckle across my nostrils.

They laughed, the damned traitors.

"Even I know that's not how it'd pan out, pretty boy." Cu walked past me, jarring his shoulder into mine.

I frowned, brushing dirt from my sleeve. "Any ideas on others we could recruit?"

"I may have one or two folks in mind. I'll send out ravens tomorrow." Mave put her hands on her hips.

"You do realize you can send electronic mail now?" I asked.

"Can electronic mail go all the way to the celestial planes?" Mave gave a smug grin. "Besides, you're the one that insists on using that archaic pager."

"Alright, send word to anyone you think may wish to help. We've stalled the Dullahan long enough. Seeing that he brought Balor back means we've run out of options. Time to take this to the next level." I crouched, picked up a brown stone the same shade as Abby's eyes, and tossed it around in my palm.

"I'm starvin'. Contact me when you know our next move." Cu huffed and disappeared into the trees.

"I'll let you know once I've heard back from them." Mave turned to leave but paused when she saw me unmoving. "Are you gonna stay here in the middle of the woods?" Her hand flittered, referencing the forest surrounding us.

"I *am* a Druid. Here is where I feel most at home." It wasn't a complete lie. The entirety of my power derived from whatever Mother Nature provided. I had no choice but to make it my home.

Mave nodded, a knowing grin spreading over her lips. "Uh-huh. Tell her I said 'Hi'." She winked before sauntering away.

I forced a smile, waving at her. Once I could no longer make out her form within the trees, I closed my eyes and steadied my breathing. Making mental contact with someone so far away took immense concentration. It wasn't as exhausting as contacting someone who'd passed into the Otherworld but I *did* manage to do that once.

Abby. Can ya hear me?

I projected my thoughts to her, my brow straining as I waited for a response. Rather than her calming, feminine voice gracing my ears, I could only hear a faint buzzing sound. Widening my stance, I focused all my energy.

Abby? Where are you?

Still just the faint buzzing sound and the wind rustling through the leaves around me. I opened my eyes, rubbing my lips together, tasting the Earth. A pit formed in my stomach, my mind betraying me, immediately jumping to the worst conclusion. Either she was in trouble, or I'd just received the equivalent of a mental slap to the face.

3

ERIMON

"WELL, I, FOR ONE, AM not going up there. No bleedin'
way," Mave said, turning her back on me.

"You? I probably won't even fit in these pint-sized dwellings,"
Cu added, flicking his wrist at the building.

Mave rolled her eyes. "If Finn can fit, you certainly can, you
big oaf."

Cu poked himself in the chest and leaned into Mave's face.
"He's not *that* much wider than me."

"Who said anything about wide?" Mave flashed him a
cheeky grin.

We stood outside an apartment building in New York
City made of aged, red brick. It looked dilapidated, with the
occasional boarded window, half-broken porches, and chunks
missing from corners here and there. It unsettled me that *this*
was Abby's apartment building. I'd told them where we were
going; they'd stick out like a sore thumb if they didn't wear
different clothes. Did they listen? Of course, they didn't.

"I can't leave you all standin' here on the sidewalk looking like a damned Renaissance Fair." I pressed my palms together and then dragged one hand over my hair, rubbing the back of my head.

A woman walked by in a black trench coat, hair pulled into a ponytail, and sunglasses that covered half of her face. She scrunched her nose as she passed, the large bag draped over her forearm swaying.

I flashed a charming, squinty-eyed smile and waved at her. "Top 'o the mornin' to ye." The woman's brows shot up, and picking up her pace, dashed around the corner. I frowned. The accent and cliché lines always seemed to break the ice with strangers in the past.

"What is a Reconnaissance Fair?" Maved asked, paying no mind to the frightened woman who'd just scurried away.

I dragged a hand over my face and beard. "It's *Renaissance*. It's a fair where people dress as medieval—" I started, but stopped when I saw their perplexed expressions. "Never mind. You're both coming up, and you'll stay in the hallway while I talk to her, deal?"

"I'm good with it. Always wanted to see you get punched in the face by a woman," Cu strolled past, slipping a toothpick into his mouth and rolling it between his teeth.

I guffawed. "Abby wouldn't punch me."

"How long have you been around again?" Mave bumped her shoulder into mine as she passed.

"Long enough," I said through gritted teeth.

"And human women—been around a lot of those?" Mave asked, twirling some of her red hair with her finger.

I rolled my shoulders. "Let's get this over with." Cracking my neck, I let out a deep sigh.

We stepped into the elevator inside, Cu being the last to board. He had to duck and crane his neck to the side to fit, the elevator bobbing and creaking in protest. Mave grabbed onto the sidewall with her hand, her other grasping the hilt of her sword.

"Is it supposed to do that?" Mave asked, widening her stance like she'd just experienced an earthquake.

I shrugged, reaching forward to press number eight on the panel. "That depends. Do you imagine we all weigh more than a hundred and fifty stones?" A sly grin tugged at my lips at the sight of Mave squirming. Who'd have thought the tough warrior-ess would be afraid of elevators?

"Cu weighs half of that on his own." Mave widened her stance even more, pressing both hands against opposite walls, pushing herself into a corner.

The doors *binged* open, and I stepped out, chuckling to myself. "It baffles me that none of you have ever bothered to step outside the celestial until I called on you in Ireland. There is an entire galaxy out there, ya know?"

Cu strolled out, followed by Mave, who sprinted and yelped as the doors began to close.

"The celestial is a galaxy all of its own. Don't need to be meddlin' my brain with more than one." Cu grumbled, canting his head from left to right, and stretching his arms skyward.

The sound of breaking glass put me on alert. Mave stood in the hallway with an axe and a broken firebox on the wall next to her. She released a hearty laugh, twirling it in her hands, before giving it a swing. "I, for one, love this world. They've got axes on the walls for anyone to grab and use in battle."

I scratched the back of my head, storming over and ripping the axe from her hands. Ignoring her scowl, I placed the axe back into its compartment. With a wiggle of my fingers, all of the glass fragments floated, and I opened my hand, piecing them back together, and secured the entire sheet of glass. "It's not there for anyone to use, Mave. It's for the people that fight fires." Exactly how old was this building to still have axes on the walls? After this was over, I fully planned to convince Abby to move in with *me*.

"How is an axe going to take out a fire?" Cu's face scrunched, and he shook his head.

I left that one alone and herded them to the corner of the hallway. "Can you both stay here and touch absolutely nothin'?" Mave nodded her head once, and Cu grunted. "Nothin'." I pointed at Cu in particular.

"We got it. We got it, loverboy. Get on with it." Cu flicked his hand toward the hall.

As I walked, I took several deep breaths before standing in front of her door. I ran my hands in succession several times over my beard before touching my fingertips to the wood grain. She was home. Her presence radiated from inside, pulsing through the wood, tugging at my insides. I let my hand fall, staring at the door like it was about to explode in my face. What the hell was I doing? I'm Erimon, son of Mil Espaine the conqueror. And yet, I let the notion of Abby's reaction cause me hesitation.

Tightening my jaw, I beat my fist against the door. While

waiting, I rolled my shoulders back, clasping my hands in front of me. Then I casually leaned against the doorframe, summoning my best smolder, and shook my head at myself, standing upright and normal. The door opened, and all the air escaped my lungs. There stood Abby—*my* Abby—those long, wavy, dark tendrils of hair falling over her shoulders and breasts.

Her eyes were wide with shock, and she stood frozen. Seeing her and the Celtic tattoo traveling down the length of her arm made my trousers tighten. I shifted my stance, lifting my palms cautiously like I would with a wild stallion. I tested a step forward, keeping an eye on her face. The shock melted away, replaced with a scowl I'd only seen her give the Dullahan. *Shite.*

"Do you have *any* idea what I've been through?" Her petite bicep tensed as her grip tightened on the door, and her chest began to heave.

And *why* was she wearing—oven mitts?

After taking a moment to appreciate the way her breasts looked in that low-cut shirt, I pressed my palms together, taking another step forward. Was this a trick question? "Abby, I'm sorry. I had no idea I'd be this long, but we ran into… complications."

"Complications?" She crossed her arms, causing her breasts to push together, and I fought every compulsion not to glance down again.

A giant fist clocked me in the jaw, sending me stumbling sideways. Glowering and rubbing my chin, I turned to a very pissed Finn looming over me.

"I second that. What kind of bleedin' complications, Monny?"

Finn unclenched and re-clenched his fists.

Still rubbing my very sore jaw, I frowned at him. "Firstly, ow. And secondly, will you two give me a chance to explain?"

They both went silent, glaring at me with mirroring imposing poses with arms tightly crossed over their chests.

I scratched my cheek, averting my gaze to look around her apartment. It was simpler than I'd imagined and *tiny*. I'd spend half my time here trying not to bump into anything. A small kitchen was in the corner with a stove and mint green refrigerator that looked a hundred years old. The living room had an area rug in the center with a bright, flowered pattern composed of blues and greens. There was a two-seat, blue couch with a purple blanket draped over it, and I couldn't tell where she would sleep for the life of me.

"Yeah, we made it to the barrier of the Otherworld just as we planned, but when we attempted to break the Ninth Wave, we ran into *complications*." I rushed my words to get to more pressing matters. "More importantly. How are *you*?" A soft smile tugged at my mouth, and I attempted to take another step forward. "Were you baking?" I pointed at the mittens.

She retreated backward, her lips thinning, but I caught her eyes dropping to my mouth for a fraction of a second. "How am I? I almost caught my apartment on fire. *That's* how I am, Erimon."

"And me," Finn added, jutting a thumb at himself.

My smile turned into a frown. "Wait, what? Did you leave a pot on the stove?" I winced, the words spewing before I could process them.

Her arms flew into the air. "No!" She stormed to the other

side of the apartment—under a meter away. "I woke up to the sunrise and caught these on fire, Erimon." Abby lifted half-burnt sunflower curtains from a trash bin, still using—the mittens.

"And me," Finn added again.

My brows cinched together. "When did this happen?"

"Yesterday." She sniffled.

I snapped my fingers. "That explains the lack of fireballs. I told Mave that it had never happened before. Wait until she hears—" I'd been smiling at first, but it soon disappeared when I caught sight of Abby.

She sniffled again, and her bottom lip quivered, her face scrunching.

My heart fell to my feet, and I lessened the distance between us in two quick steps. "Are you—please tell me you're not about to—" I touched her arm like it may have burned me. This Druid warrior had few weaknesses—decapitation, a well-made Sheperd's Pie, and women crying.

She burst into tears, slapping her hands over her face, her shoulders bouncing.

"You're an eejit. Now you went and made your woman cry, Druid." Finn rubbed Abby's shoulders.

The pain twisted my heart like wringing out a wet towel. Seeing a woman weep was terrible enough, but *this* woman? I didn't wait for an invitation, reaching my arms out to her and pulling her against me after Finn reluctantly let go. Abby's tears seeped into my shirt, and she clutched the collar of my jacket. She didn't pull away, so I continued to hold her, my jaw clenching so fiercely my teeth could've cracked.

I sniffed the air. That's odd. Smoke? I hadn't seen a fireplace in her apartment, not like there'd be any room for it—no lit candles. I sniffed again, a radiating heat growing on my shoulder.

"Oh my God," Abby screamed, backing away from me, the mittens clasped over her mouth, one burnt so profusely I could see her bare hand through it.

Flickers of orange danced from the corner of my eye. In a flash, I ripped the jacket off, throwing it to the floor. Using my boot, I stomped the flame until nothing but tendrils of grey smoke remained. Abby had pushed herself into a corner where the sunlight couldn't hit her, and I hadn't the heart to remind her yet that the sun was *always* out. She gripped each side of her head, breathing growing erratic.

Finn and I walked over to her, our hands outstretched. She shook her head frantically, backing against the wall as far as it would let her.

"Abby, it's alright. I put it out. See? No harm done. Not that you could hurt me anyway, right?" I gave a cocky grin, hoping somehow, it'd make her smile or roll her eyes for all I cared. At this point, I just wanted her to calm down.

"We haven't left the apartment since yesterday, Monny. She's been too afraid she'd catch some innocent passerby on fire." Finn said gruffly, hesitantly resting a large hand atop Abby's head, and when she let him, he stroked her hair.

The problem was, she could've very well done that. Fuck.

"And I wasn't here to help you through it like I promised. I know, but I'm here now, and I'll teach you how to control it. Everything will be right as rain." Until I told them that not only was the Dullahan an issue, but Balor was now as well—a conversation for another time.

She sniffled, running the back of her hand across her nose. Even with eyes and nostrils reddened from crying, she remained as gorgeous as ever. Finn backed away, but gazed at Abby like a concerned uncle.

Crouching, I opened my arms to her again. She lowered her hands, eyeing my welcoming posture, a tiny smile cresting her lips. And then it melted into *fury.*

"You haven't contacted me in *weeks.*" She held up her right hand with the Claddagh ring I'd given her as a means of magical telephone.

I let my arms fall slack at my sides and rubbed the back of my head. "I figured you didn't want to talk to me, so I left ye alone."

Her jaw dropped, and she let out a noise that sounded like an angry feline. It made my entire body tense. "Because I wanted *you* to reach out to me." Her voice shook as if she were about to start crying again.

Mave was right. There'd be no living with her after this. I formed my eyes into slits. "Do you *also* want to punch me?"

Finn nodded at her vigorously.

Her mouth formed a tiny 'o'. "What?"

I stood, playing with the rings on my fingers before pulling at the hem of my tank top. "Punch me. It might make ye feel better?"

She stared at me, possibly contemplating my offer. "I'm mad at you. That doesn't mean I want to punch you."

And now something to rub in Cu's face. I smiled and squinted my eyes, a look I knew always made her knees wobble. Leaning forward, I played with the rings on my fingers again, flexing my arms. "Not even a wee bit?"

She nibbled her lip, attempting to hide a grin. "Will you kiss me already, you crazy Druid?"

Finn scoffed in disgust and disappointment before flailing his hands at us and turning away.

A question that I finally understood. I knelt in front of her, cupped her face, and kissed her with an intensity to rival the growing fiery power in Abby's veins. Her slender arms wrapped around my neck, and she kissed me back, allowing my tongue to slip into her mouth. I pressed my growing hardness against her stomach and let out a low growl, knowing that had to wait. And it wasn't *only* because Finn was still here.

We pulled away, and I pressed my forehead against hers, closing my eyes. When I opened them, she was smiling at me, her eyes searching mine, and her grin widened.

"What you thinkin'?"

"I missed seeing that sparkle in your eyes." She ran a finger over my bearded chin, the sensation shooting straight to my groin.

I took her hand in mied, kissing the inside of her palm. "And they've missed seein' *you*."

Finn exaggerated rolling his eyes from the corner of the living room, and dropped his head in his hand.

"I'd tell you two to get a room, but I don't see one besides the one we're standin' in," Mave said from the doorway.

The door that was still very wide open. They'd heard everything. Grand.

I looked toward the ceiling, sighing. Abby leaned around me, her eyes brightening. What I wouldn't have given to see *that* reaction when she'd opened the door to see *me*. She jumped to her feet and ran past me. I turned around, my arms stiff at my sides. She wrapped her arms around Mave, hugging her.

"Thank the maker that you two showed up when you did. I damn well think they were ready to mount each other right in front of me." Finn rubbed the back of his neck.

"You came with Erimon? I'm surprised." Abby asked after spotting Cu entering.

"Does a gnome live here?" Cu asked, sneering at her apartment.

"You *both* came?" Abby asked.

"Of course, they did. Team Druid, remember?" Finn snickered, glancing toward me with a smile that suggested he'd give me more than a punch later.

"Please tell me you all didn't appear in the middle of Times Square or something? Especially dressed like that?" Abby blinked.

"Why do you think I hid them in the hallway?" I smirked and folded my arms.

"Did you get your powers yet, Abby?" Mave asked.

"I—" Abby started.

"Fire," I interjected. "Yesterday."

"Well, that'd explain the premature *extinguish*, hm?" Mave clicked her tongue against her teeth, and I narrowed my eyes.

Damn right, it does.

Cu exploded into a roar of laughter, bending over to slap a hand against his knee. "You'd think she would've gotten *that* power because she works with animals. Oh, that's bleedin' ironic."

My face fell. He had a point. I wouldn't be surprised if it were part of another cruel joke played by the very Druid who'd bestowed this gift on me thousands of years ago. I ground my teeth together before wiggling my fingers, conjuring a small sliver of the wooden floorboards to float into my hand.

"I need to teach her how to control it." I rubbed the piece of wood between my fingers.

"Is that why there's a cranium-sized hole in your jacket?" Cu asked, pointing a large hand at my tattered jacket in a slump on the floor.

I walked to Abby, running my fingertips down her arm with the tattoo. "Would you mind us stayin' here? I can't take them anywhere else without looking suspicious." Her apartment was just a wee bit bigger than a broom closet, but we'd have to make it work.

"Uhhh…" She looked around at everyone before dragging some of her hair over her ear. "Sure. If you don't mind sleeping on the floor and barely moving?"

Mave pushed past everyone to the middle of the living room. "I call the gaudy rug."

"That's *my* gaudy rug. And seein' as I've been cooped here for months, I'm keeping it," Finn announced, puffing his chest at Mave.

"Fine," Mave said with a snarl.

Abby frowned. "I wouldn't call it *gaudy*."

"What would you call it, then?" Mave pointed at the rug.

Abby pursed her lips. "Vibrant?"

Mave shrugged, removing her weapons, each making a loud clank as they thudded to the floor.

Abby pinched the bridge of her nose. "Everyone, I'm on the eighth floor of this building. I have people directly below and above me. You'll have to be quieter."

Everyone grumbled and moved about the space to claim

their spots on the floor. Abby turned toward me, smiling and awkwardly rubbing her tattooed arm. I grinned, poking one of the Celtic knots within the design. "It suits you."

My own tattoo hummed now that we were in the same space again.

She slipped her hands into her back pockets. "Try explaining to everyone why you had the sudden compulsion to get a full-sleeve Celtic tattoo while vacationing in Ireland."

My chest tightened, thoroughly satiated to be in her company. "You'll have to tell me about it."

"There's *a lot* we need to talk about."

"And we will. For now, do you have a bed?" I glanced around.

She smiled, playfully slapping me on the shoulder. "Of course, I do." She walked to a side wall, slipped her hand into some hidden handle, and pulled the wall out. A bed appeared, two pegs flipping out onto the floor.

I walked over, nodding. "Magic?"

"Hardly. It's a pull-out."

Shaking my head, I eyed her sidelong. "I don't normally, no."

"What?"

I faked a cough. "Nothing."

"The bed's pretty small. We'll have to get close if both of us are going to fit." Her eyelids grew heavy, and the tip of her pink tongue wet the corner of her mouth.

"As long as I get to be the big spoon." I brushed a strand of hair from her face, my pulse quickening.

"Think you can handle that without things getting too heated?" She curled her fingers into the top of my pants.

Not if she kept doing *that*.

I flashed a sly grin. "Barely. But I'll have to make it work. Team Druid doesn't deserve *that* kind of show."

She laughed, and my soul soared. There was the version of Abby I met in Ireland—the woman I'd literally given a part of myself to. I had no idea what connection we'd have since making the transference, but given the way my body reacted to her slightest touch, I knew a lot had changed, and this was only the beginning.

4

ERIMON

THE SOUND OF A BANSHEE'S blood-curdling scream woke me from a deep sleep. I leaped from the bed, circling several times with my arms tensed and held out in front of me, ready to attack. As the sleepiness subsided from my vision, I saw—Phoebe? She and Abby hugged, bouncing up and down, and the tension eased away. I raked my fingers through my hair, suppressing a yawn, rubbing my hands down my chest and stomach.

"You were out like the dead. Mave even held a mirror up to your nose to see if you were still breathin'." Finn chuckled, sitting at the square in the corner of the space that I guessed was her dining table. It looked like a child's table compared to Finn's large form. I was surprised he could fit on the chair.

I glared at him, opening my mouth to give a witty comeback before Phoebe's shrill but lovely voice screamed, "Monny!"

Bracing for impact, I watched her scurry across the room, push from the floor, and fly straight into me. Normally, I'd have caught her with no problem but for whatever reason it was taking longer for me to wake up, and we toppled to the floor. A sea of red hair clouded my vision, her body landing on top of mine. Sputtering, I batted her hair away from my face, and all she could do was giggle.

"You're goin' to make the Chaun jealous, you know?" I cocked an eyebrow, holding her hair up and away from me with both hands.

"Nah, you're not her type," Patrick, the Leprechaun, said, peering down at me.

Phoebe smiled and playfully swatted my chest before Patrick helped her to her feet. I held my palms outward to ensure there was no accidental touching of vital body parts and stood. Abby beamed at me from across the room, twirling her dark hair between her fingers. I needed time alone with her as much as I needed air to breathe, and inwardly, it drove me mad.

"Why the hell were you gone so long?" Phoebe asked, slapping me again.

"Elder's arse, I already apologized to Abby. I didn't realize this was a threesome." I frowned, rubbing my arm in the spot she hit, pretending it hurt. In reality, it felt like a bee flew into it.

Phoebe's jaw dropped, and Abby sidled beside me, curling her arm through mine.

"Behave, you. She's my best friend and was only concerned for my well-being." Abby's eyes twinkled at me, her hand rubbing possessively at my bicep.

"Phoebe, I apologize for causin' your best lady friend any discomfort during my *unforeseen* extended absence." I placed a hand over my heart and bowed with a flourish, partially taking Abby, who was still wrapped around my arm, with me.

"Are you goin' to fill us in on what happened, or are we to guess?" Patrick asked, hugging Phoebe to his side.

Standing upright, I gave a slow nod and motioned at Mave to shut the door. "Would ye mind?"

She guffawed, her face buried in a magazine called *Cosmopolitan.* "I do mind. Close it yourself. You don't even have to walk across the room."

I opened my mouth to speak and then snapped it shut, re-evaluating my statement. "For the fortieth time, I can't move things with my mind."

Mave didn't bother to look up at me, flipping through the magazine, pausing to stick her nose against one of the pages, sniffing. "Tell that to the dozen doors I've seen you splinter."

My jaw clenched several times, and Abby's grip tightened on my arm, obviously sensing my growing tension. "Yes, but I'd have to disassemble only to reassemble —you know, what?" I stormed across the room, Abby letting go of me. With the door firmly in my grasp, I aimed to slam it shut, but halfway there remembered Abby's pleas to keep quiet, and the slam turned into a delicate click. I turned around, rolling my shoulders, and gave as calming of an expression as I could manage. Judging by the looks on everyone's faces, my calming face more resembled that I wished to punch a hole in the drywall.

"There's not a whole lot to be said. Except for Balor, that is." Cu grunted, leaning the chair back on two legs.

"Balor? What do ye mean, Balor?" Patrick's arms unfolded, and he took a step forward.

"Perhaps we should have built up to that part, Cu. Hm?" I raised my brows and moved to the middle of the room.

"We fought the Dullahan on the next full moon and lured him to the gateway of the Otherworld. We were close, ever so close to breaking the Ninth Wave, the Dullahan in our clutches, bound by those same golden shackles, and the *Femori* attacked." Absently, I twisted the rings on my fingers, recalling that day.

"Femori?" Phoebe asked, looking at Patrick as if a leprechaun would've ever come face to face with one.

"Sea monsters," I answered before the Chaun had a chance to make something up to impress his blushing bride.

"Oh, don't undersell it, Erimon." Mave finally glanced up from her lady articles, slapping the magazine shut. "Fierce, vile creatures, the Femori are. Teeth as sharp as the sharpest knives, fingers long and deadly, and their screams cause even the fiercest immortals to cower."

Cu smirked, rocking back and forth on the chair legs that I secretly hoped would break and send him to his ass. "Speak for yourself, witch. You were the one whose ears bled."

"And you conveniently had clay to stuff in *your* ears. Gods know where ye pulled that out from," Mave said, narrowing her eyes at Cu.

Raising my voice a decibel, "The Femori are controlled by Balor, who is one of the gods of death, although he's so arrogant, he calls himself *the* God of Death."

"I thought the Dullahan was the god of death," Abby asked.

"Balor was killed eons ago by his grandson, and so Balor's charge of death fell into the Dullahan's lap. Before that, he was a grim reaper, if you will," Mave said, finding the convenience to stand from her chair.

"And now, with Balor back, the Dullahan's previous job is

reinstated, and they've joined forces." I sniffed once, scratching the side of my nose. Averting my gaze elsewhere, I waited for this realization to sink in with Abby and Phoebe.

Abby took calculated steps toward me, steadily raising a hand. "So, let me get this straight. Not only do we have the Dullahan, who is the *grim reaper*, to contend with, but now the god of death and his pointy teeth sea creatures too?"

"Yes." I grimaced, unable to meet her gaze right away.

"What?" Abby's eyes bulged out of her skull, her arms tense at her sides.

Crackling sounds followed by a loud *bang* vibrated the floorboards. Everyone's heads whipped in that direction only to find Cu with his arse on the floor and a broken chair. This didn't seem to faze Abby, who still stood frozen, her eyes wide and body tense. I moved to her side and cupped her elbow, using a single finger to trace her tattoo.

"Abby, we'll get past this." I tilted my head and squeezed her arm for reassurance.

Fear transformed into fierce determination, her jaw tightening. "Teach me how to use this power. I'm not cowering behind a rock this time around."

My chest tightened, and I slid my hand from her elbow up her arm and caressed her cheek. I'd have been lying to myself if I said I didn't want to protect her, lock her in a room even, to keep her from harm's way. That wasn't Abby, though. It never had been. "And I won't ask you to."

There was a loud *thud* from a window behind us, making Abby jump. A large, black bird repeatedly thumped against the glass, squawking.

"What in the world?" Abby asked, scurrying over.

It could've been anyone or anything. I'd seen far too many shapeshifters in my time to assume an animal was what it appeared to be. "Abby, don't. Remember the kelpie?" An angelic white horse who lured people with its beauty to the river's edge only to drag them into the water and feast on their entrails. That particular kelpie also happened to have been an ex-conquest.

"If it keeps flying into the window like that, it's going to kill itself. I don't care who or what it is." Abby flicked the lock for the windows, and the bird flew in, falling to the ground in exhaustion.

"That's probably the raven I sent. Surprised it's back already," Finn said, pushing from the wall he'd been leaning on.

"Poor thing," Abby yelped, not hesitating to scoop the raven into her arms.

The raven squawked so loudly it made my ears ring. Abby petted its head, making shushing sounds. Despite her best efforts, the bird wasn't having it. Patiently, I gave a few more moments to see if Abby could soothe it with her zoological skills despite my ear drums rattling. When the winged beast showed no signs of stopping, I gingerly ran my hand down its head and the length of its back. It gave one final caw before nestling into Abby's arms.

Her mouth fell slack. "I don't think I'll ever get tired of watching you do that."

Showing off had always been one of my more negative qualities, admittedly. But showing off for *Abby*, I'd never get enough of it. I flashed a smile, moving my hand from the raven to graze my fingers up her tattooed arm.

"Would you two mind if I cut in?" Finn asked, looming over us with his hands on his hips.

We exchanged bewildered looks until Finn nonchalantly motioned with his finger at the small piece of parchment dangling from a string around the bird's neck. Abby untied the paper and handed it to Finn, his large hand making the note look the size of a Post-It when, in actuality, it was the size of a regular sheet of paper.

Finn's caterpillar eyebrows furrowed as he read the letter before raising it above his head. "I got us another member for our band, ladies and lads."

"Who, pray tell?" Mave asked.

"Morrigan," Finn answered with a smile as wide as his head.

The room fell silent for undoubtedly different reasons. The immortals knew Morrigan as The Phantom Queen, a goddess synonymous with battle. She'd been known to cause men to go into a war frenzy a time or two, and though none of us considered her to be good nor evil, it was questionable which version you'd get on any given day.

"Are ye daft?" Patrick asked. "You can't trust that woman. Not to mention, she's a shapeshifter. She could be *that* raven for all we know." He pointed at the bird in Abby's arms, and Abby stiffened.

"It's not her. She normally shifts into a crow if it's a bird." Cu added, still sitting on the chair that collapsed to the floor. Cu stared in front of him, his hands clenched. All color drained from his face, and if I hadn't known better, I'd say he looked *scared*.

"Cu, why do you look like someone pissed in your Guinness?" I asked, half afraid of the answer.

Mave grinned, sliding forward until she stood in front of Cu, tapping her fingernails against her armor. "He tried to kill her. Didn't ye, hound boy?"

Cu's expression melted into panic and then anger before he pointed a finger at Mave. "It wasn't that simple. She wanted me in her bed, but I refused, and for that, she made the Cattle Raid of Cooley a living nightmare. What was I supposed to do? Let her kill me and my men?" He dragged a hand over his face. "Besides, I *did* give her a blessing that healed her wounds."

Mave bounced her knees, still grinning like a jackal. "You didn't know it was her."

Cu growled and slammed his fists against the floor. "Shut up, geebag."

"Why in the shite did you deny her advances?" I asked, genuinely perplexed.

Cu mumbled under his breath and stood. "Some of us warriors have more on our minds than what's between a woman's legs, *Druid*."

Still perplexed.

"I take it you haven't seen her since this little squabble?" Phoebe's small voice chimed in.

"No," Cu grumbled. "And it's been *nice*." He turned his glare on Finn.

"She's not coming *here,* is she?" Abby asked, clutching the raven to her chest.

I ground my molars, my brain going into overdrive. "No. No, she won't. Because Finn, Mave, and Cu are all going to go back to Ireland and wait for her there. Right?"

As if their heads were all on swivels, they turned to glare at me.

"You drag us all the way here, and now you want us to go?" Finn asked.

Forcing a chuckle, I flashed a sparkling smile toward Abby and crossed the room to my three mythical companions. "Look, we can't bring beings like that here. Go. Back. We'll meet up with you in a few days," I whispered.

Mave tapped her foot, and I glanced down before looking back to her face with a shrug. "What now?"

"Can I say one more thing?" Mave held a finger up, *still* grinning.

Sighing, I made a hurry-up gesture.

"I invited Rhiannon to fight with us." Mave paused, looking at a disgruntled Cu out of the corner of her eye. "And she accepted."

Cu kicked the air. "You've got to be fucking kidding me."

"What's the issue now?" Patrick asked.

Finn clapped Patrick on the back, making him stumble forward. "Morrigan and Rhiannon don't get along in the slightest. They're like oil and water."

"To put it mildly," I add, shaking my head.

Mave chuckled and shrugged. "How would I have known who Finn was bringing?"

"Alright, look. It's going to be fine. Everything will be grand. We'll figure it out in Ireland. Now, all of you *go*." I swept them toward the door.

"Are you forgetting the only way we can get back is by you? Or did ye want us to catch the next flight out?" Mave's foot tapped against the floorboards.

My face fell, and I sighed, gazing toward the heavens. Mave's constant rightness surely couldn't be a habit. "Abby,

I'll be back in two, three seconds. Promise." I turned toward them, hurriedly huddling them together.

"Last time you said that, I didn't see you for months," Abby's voice cut deep into my chest.

I tensed, looking at the surprised expressions given by my counterparts. Over my shoulder, Abby stood rigid, stroking the bird's feathers, a plea for me to stay dancing in her gaze. I held one finger up at the three of them before making my way over to her, lightly placing my hands on each of her arms.

"That was different. I'm only poppin' them back to the Motherland." I stared at her, tilting my head to the side, studying her expression.

"Erimon, if you don't come back right away, so help me—"

I pressed a chaste kiss to her lips, and she sighed against my mouth.

Once her eyes fluttered open, she pursed her lips. "Damn you." Then, there was a subtle hint of a smile.

I held up five fingers. "Five seconds, tops."

"You just said two to three seconds."

Tilting my head, I squinted. "I'm givin' myself a few extra seconds in case I trip or something."

She rolled her eyes and motioned toward everyone behind me with her chin. "Go. Before Morrigan shows up in the middle of Central Park."

I gave her one last squeeze before turning, holding my arms out to my sides, and wrapped them around Finn before he had a chance to protest. He'd always hated porting. It made him sick even, but we didn't have time for anything else. Cu and Mave grabbed onto my shoulders, and *pop* we went.

We appeared in the middle of the woods beneath a large canopy of leaves, and I furrowed my brow. This didn't seem right. I'd intended for us to appear by Patrick's hovel. I wasn't even sure if we were in Ireland.

"Why'd ye take us here?" Finn asked, scratching the back of his head and doing several turns.

"I didn't. I'm not sure where *here* is." Tugging at my jacket collar, I closed my eyes, letting my powers take over. Willing nature to speak to me, whisper to me where we were.

The ground vibrated, and I opened one eye, knowing I wasn't the cause. Smoke billowed around us like a grey blanket, swirling. A giant black horse charged through the blur of fog. Its nostrils spewed fire, and seated upon its saddle was the Dullahan himself *sans* shackles larger, and more fearsome than I'd ever seen him. He swung the black human spine whip in a circle over his head, giving it a loud *crack*.

Abby was going to have my *hide*.

5

ABBY

WHEN ERIMON HAD *NOT* RETURNED in the five seconds he promised, I went silent, moved to my living room window, without sunflower curtains now, and distracted myself with the New York City skyline. Patrick and Phoebe stayed with me, and Phoebe, uncharacteristically mature for her, let me wander off to deal with it the way I needed. I still cradled the raven in my arms because I hadn't the heart to let it fly away until I knew it wouldn't injure itself. I stroked its soft feathers, and it let out the occasional tiny cawing sound.

"How long has it been?" I asked no one in particular.

"Thirty minutes," Phoebe's soft voice answered.

Patrick appeared from the corner of my eye and leaned near the window. "Look, you know I'm never one to give an ounce of credit to the damn Druid, but I assure ye, he's not doing it on purpose. His life is very unpredictable."

"It's not that, Patrick." I'd gotten so close to the glass that my words created a sheet of fog on it. "I'm worried about him. Especially when I can't hear him, and I'm realizing that if I want to be with him, I'll have to learn to cope with it." Frowning, I drew a trinity knot before the fog disappeared.

Patrick nodded before elbowing me, garnering my attention. "There's a reason that mythical beings, deities, creatures, don't find love easily, if at all." He looked saddened initially, but his face brightened once he caught sight of Phoebe across the room.

"Immortality?" I rested the raven on the couch, testing to see if it'd try to fly away. He lifted his wings slightly and made circles on the cushion before motionlessly perching as if content.

"Not necessarily. Immortality brings eternity, but long-lasting love doesn't require it." Patrick held his palm out, a single gold coin dropping from an invisible pocket in the air. He flipped it over his knuckles as he continued. "It's the demanding lives we lead. And they're demanding because of these chimerical existences we've been blessed with. Nothing comes without consequence—magic most of all."

Without Erimon within celestial reach, I developed an unfathomable pain in my chest. I'd never felt anything quite as tingly mixed with a dull ache that intensified the more I thought about him. I pressed my palms to the wall, steadying my breathing, but the bond was relentless, and soon my skin *burned*.

"Abby, is it supposed to be doing that?" Phoebe asked.

When I opened my eyes, she'd been pointing at my tattoo, and I reeled back on my heels. The tattoo glowed orange, red, and tinges of blue beneath my skin. It scorched a heated pattern through the infinite design like it was trying to find an escape.

"I think I need to get rid of it somehow. But I don't know how big of a flame it'll be or where to—" I eyed my oven and ran to it. "Patrick, open the door. Phoebe, there's an extinguisher in the pantry. I don't know what else to do." The heat pricked at my skin, and I hissed, wincing back the pain radiating through my arm. "But I can't take it anymore."

Phoebe ran into the kitchen with the extinguisher ready while Patrick stood with his hand on the oven handle, waiting for my word.

"Now," I shouted. Once the door opened, I hurled my hand into it, shooting a swirling mix of fire and embers. It was like iced tea on a humid summer day or a steaming hot shower in the middle of winter—relief and comfort.

My hand dropped limp at my side, spent, and Phoebe did a couple of quick spurts to ensure the flames were sufficiently squelched. I trailed my fingers down the tattoo that had returned to normal and sighed. "Is it so much to ask that the Dullahan give me a month or so before trying to claim my soul again?" Somehow, I found the humor in such a plea and chuckled.

"Maybe you should wear gloves?" Phoebe suggested, still holding the extinguisher.

"More like a full-body fire suit. Who's to say the only harm comes from my hands? And the oven mittens only worked for a *day*." I flopped onto the sofa, propping my feet on the coffee table and rubbing my temples. "It's going to be alright. I already feel a bit more accustomed to it, and Erimon will teach me the rest. Soon." Twirling the Claddagh ring on my finger, I sucked in a quick breath.

Very soon.

The raven cawed and waddled across the cushion until he stood on my lap. His glossy black eyes peered at me as he tilted his head from side to side.

"Looks like you have a new pet," Phoebe said, grinning and offering her knuckles for the bird to rub its crest against them.

"No, no. I'm only watching him until I can make sure he's able to fly on his own again." I scratched behind the raven's head.

Patrick propped his arms on the couch's back. "I don't know. He looks pretty content where he is."

"If you were going to keep him, hypothetically speaking, what would you name him?" Phoebe tapped a finger against her lips. "Caw-Caw? Simone? Oh, Sir Feathers?"

Typically, I'd give my best friend a perplexed expression toward her odd choices, but my mind remained focused on the bird and the one name that came to me without thought or hesitation.

"Emrys," I announced.

The raven fanned his wings and lifted its beak as if in agreement.

"Emrys," Phoebe repeated. "I like that. A beautiful name for a beautiful bird."

Patrick's eyes sparkle, and he gave me a dimpled grin. "The one without end."

Eternity.

Frowning, I turned on the couch to face Patrick and Phoebe, a knot lodging in my throat preventing me from speaking at first. "He *has* been gone awhile. And given he promised, there's only one thing I could imagine that's making him break it."

"The Dullahan," we said in unison, exchanging worried glances.

But here I was, unable to help, unable to do a damned thing but wait. The Dullahan needed to be stopped, not only to save me from death but because I was ready to move on with this new part of my life and have grown tired of fucking *waiting*.

6

ERIMON

I DROPPED TO ONE KNEE with a grunt, slamming my fist into the dirt and flaring my falcon wings. The ground shook, a crack forming, until it reached the horse, and a pointed rock thrust from beneath, clipping the black beast in the chest. The horse neighed in protest, the smoke from its nose intensifying, the red of its eyes blazing.

"If your goal were to piss him off further, I'd say you're doin' a bang-up job," Finn grumbled, removing the hilt of his fog sword from his shirt.

A growl vibrated in my throat. "I don't have time for this."

"And *we* do?" Mave asked, unsheathing her blade.

"I say we go for a record," Cu said, cracking his neck.

"A record?" Finn cocked a bushy eyebrow.

"How long it takes us to send him running away with his whip between his legs," Cu responded, his body morphing into the hulking creature that'd deliver a warp-spasm.

"An extra-large pint of Guinness to whoever makes this thorn in my paw disappear," I spat and stomped the ground with my boot. Rocks launched skyward from beneath the horse, causing it to rear up on its hind legs, its hooves frantically punching the air in front of it.

Finn let out a hearty chuckle, the fog blade forming on his sword. "I would've done it for free."

"I needed a good stretch," Mave said, twirling her sword and cracking her neck.

Cu charged the horse from its side, slamming his giant fist into its ribs. The impact made the animal topple but not fall, Dullahan striking Cu's shoulder with the tip of the spine whip. It slashed a line of crimson, and Cu roared, taking labored steps to the nearest tree and ripping the trunk from its roots.

I grimaced, the sight of the plant's lifelines being severed surging an irritating sting down my spine. Shoving the pain aside, I splayed my palms at my sides, calling shards of bark to me, which I fully intended to return. But for now, they served as natural daggers to repeatedly throw at the death god.

Cu swung the tree like a hammer, missing once, twice, and a third time from his slower gait in this titanic form. It slammed into the Dullahan's back on the fourth pass, sending him catapulting to the ground. The horse dug its hooves into the dirt, smoke wafting from its nostrils, eyes blazing red flames. The Dullahan roared before floating to his feet, snapping the whip with a skeletal hand.

Finn approached me with his sword raised, and without taking his eyes from the death god he asked, "Is it just me, or does he seem unusually quiet?"

"Or—" I slammed my boot in the dirt, causing a spike in the

ground which jabbed Dullahan in the gut, sending him straight back to his ass. "—he needs to concentrate this time around."

Snarling, The Dullahan pulled himself to his feet, a rusting and withered scythe appearing in his other hand. "Idiots."

"That got his attention," I said to Finn, smiling.

A flock of dozens of crows flew overhead, darkening the sky and blotting out the sun. Cu stopped dead in his tracks, his hulking form staring upward before slowly materializing into his more human self. The crows formed a spiraling trail, edging closer until they blended together. After several caws and blackened wings flapping, the crows were gone, and the Phantom Queen stood in their place.

Morrigan.

Morrigan's emerald eyes played on the Dullahan, her midnight black hair with tints of crimson falling to her hips, fluttering in a non-existent breeze. "The only true imbecile I see here, Crom, is *you.*"

"I am simply doing my divine duty. It is not my concern for those who cannot accept it." The Dullahan rested his whip over his shoulder, leaning both hands on the scythe's handle.

Morrigan clicked her long, black nails together, the silver circlet adorning her forehead glinting from the sun's rays, animated smoke floating at its edges. "You truly are dense if you're trying to trick *me.* I see all. And you're attempting to derail fate, despite the constant cosmic warnings."

"I was drawn to her. She is to die. Even *you* cannot deny this."

Morrigan paused, her gaze flicking suddenly to my wings folded behind me. "Those are new." A sensual smile tilted her lips, her fingers wriggling as if she wished to touch them.

Holding up a palm, I made the wings momentarily disappear. "Put it back in your trousers, Mor. I'm spoken for."

"Yes." Morrigan glanced at Finn, who nodded at her, and then her attention turned back to the Dullahan. "So, I've heard. It makes little sense to me why you bother to fight when a full moon puts you at heightened strength."

An eerily deep chuckle escaped Dullahan's throat, and his bony hands wrung the scythe's handle. "This was not about fighting."

My blood, my mind, my everything froze.

"I lured you here to give time for Balor to find Miss Weber." He continued to laugh, raspy and sinister.

Fuck.

But he didn't know Abby had changed. Not even Morrigan knew.

"And how in the dubnos does he plan to do that? It's a big world out there, Dully," Finn said, still standing ready with his fog sword.

"I absorbed enough of her essence the last time I had thought I killed her, enabling us to track the mortal. And you have all used up your parlor tricks to revive her a second time. She is still mortal, after all." The last words rolled from the Dullahan's tongue like poison.

"As far as you know," I seethed.

The Dullahan's hooded head shook from left to right. "It does not matter. Soon, she will be trapped until the next moon, and I will not have wasted precious hours searching for her. It will be done then and there. And you, Druid, cannot get to her."

This wasn't right. None of it. Why couldn't I hear her? All I needed was one whisper, and I could be there in an instant.

"Can't he?" Morrigan asked, arching a dark brow and an ethereal wind drafted through her ashen robes.

Eternity.

Abby's sweet and sultry voice echoed in my head like a soothing lullaby, and the tattoo *burned* against my skin.

Spreading a wide grin, I snapped my fingers. "This'll take but a moment."

In the split instance it took for me to port away from the woods, I could hear the Dullahan's wails of protest and the steed's hooves charging forward. But in the next breath, I appeared in Abby's apartment, where she sat on the couch, holding something. Patrick and Phoebe were at the kitchenette table. There wasn't time for an explanation. By the time Abby turned to see me, my arms were already around her.

"Patrick, take Phoebe and get out of here, now," I commanded.

Not risking Balor being at her doorstep, I whisked us back to the woods where I'd left my motley crew.

7

ABBY

I'D BEEN QUIETLY STROKING EMRYS' feathers when Erimon appeared. I didn't have the chance to feel elated to see him or even confused because no sooner had he arrived than he ported us away, shouting at Patrick for them to leave. I stood dumbfounded in the middle of the woods in my tank top, yoga pants, and flip flops, clutching Emrys to my chest.

"Ah, the lady of the hour," a woman with black hair said, her lips curving into a smile.

The tattoo hummed in delight with Erimon a breath away from me, and it calmed my bubbling nerves. "Erimon—"

"Wait, Abby. I know. It was the Dullahan." Erimon's hands found my shoulders, rubbing them.

"Where is he?" I scanned the surrounding trees, examining Finn and Mave.

Erimon cursed in Gaelic. "Conveniently not here, but I swear he was right before I left."

"Morrigan frightened him off. Threatened him and the

like," Finn added, bobbing his bushy brows.

Morrigan. I turned my gaze on the woman with black hair. The only one I hadn't recognized.

"Is that the same raven?" Erimon asked, finally noticing Emrys nestled into the crook of my arm.

"I didn't want to let him go until I knew he wasn't injured. But when I tried to free him, he refused to leave."

Emrys squawked and tilted his head at Erimon, clacking his black tongue against his beak.

"It's because he's drawn to you. Drawn to a Bandruí." Morrigan took graceful steps toward me until we stood a foot away from each other.

Without asking, I offered Emrys to Erimon to hold. Erimon didn't hesitate, taking the bird in his arm and trailing a finger up and down its back.

I offered my hand to her. "Morrigan, I take it?"

"That's right." She shook it and held on for a moment longer, her gaze roaming my Celtic tattoo. "It's nice to finally meet you, Abby."

"Finally?" I asked.

She canted her head, not answering my confused expression. "The Bandruí are in a similar realm as witches. Mortals of this variety have sought my guidance for centuries. I'd be happy to do the same for you if you so wish."

This woman, this goddess, was beautiful—high cheekbones, a perfectly proportionate width and slant to her nose, a complexion between pale and tanned.

"Now, now, Mor, she's Druid first. I have to show her how to use the fire she's inherited, and then if she wants, you can show her the ways of the Bandruí, but one step at a time, yeah?" Erimon pressed a hand at the small of my back.

A glint formed in Morrigan's eyes, an understanding smile following. "Of course. But Abby, know that your magic could go beyond fire alone if you're willing to tap into it. You could be the most powerful Bandruí in history."

A breath escaped my lungs like I'd landed on my back and got the wind knocked out of me. I had no idea what to say to that and stumbled over words in my head.

"I have to say, though, I'm a bit confused," Morrigan continued, turning her attention to Erimon. "You two are bonded, but she's still mortal."

Erimon let out a raspy sigh and handed the raven back to me. "About that. The Elder is the only one that can perform the ceremony for Druids."

Morrigan nodded in understanding. "And you don't know where he is."

Coaxing Emrys to my shoulder, he happily perched there and flapped his wings.

"That's one of the reasons I asked you to help," Finn announced, moving closer.

Morrigan continued to nod, her focus mostly on me. "I agree to join you then. And don't think I haven't noticed you skulking around back there, Hound."

Cu had been halfway hiding between two trees and emerged, his hands balled into fists at his sides. "We didn't exactly leave on the best of terms the last time we saw each other. Didn't want my presence to sway your decision."

Was that something—nice, Cu just said?

Morrigan chuckled, running the Celtic knot chain necklace hanging over her chest between two fingers. "Don't flatter yourself into thinking I've still been caught up over you all these years. It's water very well and very deeply under the bridge."

"We tried to kill each other." Cu stood near Morrigan now, squinting perplexedly at her. "*Multiple* times."

"Fun, wasn't it?" Morrigan patted Cu's cheek. "And yet, here we both are."

"Having fun, are we?" A female voice that didn't belong to Mave or Morrigan asked. "I thought this was supposed to be a detrimental mission."

We turned in unison to witness a blonde woman with hair that almost looked like snow hanging past her hips seated upon a white unicorn.

Groaning, Morrigan rolled her eyes. "You failed to mention the *angel* was part of this eclectic crew."

"That was for a reason, Mor." Erimon clapped Morrigan's shoulder as he passed her. "But you've already agreed." After flashing her a coy grin, he approached the blonde woman with open arms. "Rhiannon. It's been a long time."

A long time?

My mind and gut dipped into treacherous, envious territory.

Erimon swiveled on his heel, discreetly shaking his head at me before turning his attention back to Rhiannon.

Relief settled into my bones, and I smiled to myself.

Rhiannon smiled warmly and stroked the unicorn's wheat-colored mane, several flowers braided into it. "I do have to say, Erimon, that I was pleasantly surprised by your involvement in all of this. The Druid I knew from a century ago would've made any excuse to pretend he hadn't a clue what the Dullahan's plans were and leave the mortal in the dust."

The mortal. Me.

Erimon had *not* abandoned me and did everything in his power to protect me, even when I was dying in his arms *both* times. But the idea of this other version of him made me a bit queasy. We still had so much to talk about. So much to share in a better effort to know each other. And it had to happen before I became eternally bound to him. It *had* to.

"I'm still very much the cocky, confident warrior Druid you've always known, but now with a tad more humility." Erimon held his hand out to me, guiding me to his side. "Thanks to her."

The ring vibrated against my skin, my chest tightening at his words.

Rhiannon slid from the horse, standing by it and stroking its side in her white dress with golden embroidered Celtic designs woven through it. A gold belt hung loose over her hips, a chain hanging from it with a pink metal flower at the end. Her violet eyes glanced behind us, a warm grin still gracing her lips. "Morrigan. It's *also* been a long time."

Morrigan snorted and folded her arms. "And it's been a delight."

Finn cleared his throat and slowly pushed past me and Erimon, sinking to one knee in a bow at Rhiannon's feet, his fist pressed to his chest. "Enchanting as always, my lady."

"Finn," Rhiannon whispered, placing a knuckle under his chin to lift his gaze to hers. "I'm not royalty. You've no reason to stand on ceremony with me."

Finn's cheeks turned rosy, and he gulped. "You've always been a queen to me, Rhi."

Rhiannon bent forward and placed a kiss on Finn's forehead. Finn blew out a breath and pushed to his feet, coughing and playing with the gold rings in his beard. "Glad to uh—glad to have you in our presence, my lady."

Mave narrowed her eyes at Finn when he returned. "You never bow to *me*."

"And I won't be startin', so don't get any ideas."

Cu pointed between Morrigan and Rhiannon. "Are you two going to be a problem?"

"No, they won't," Erimon answered. "Isn't that right, Mor?"

Morrigan floated on grey smoky tendrils until she was nose to nose with Rhiannon. "There won't be a problem so long as Miss Goody Good doesn't stop me from doing what I must."

Rhiannon slipped a hand to Morrigan's shoulder, and she shrugged it away. "Someone needs to keep this group righteous. Because if it were up to you, you'd simply murder your way through it."

"I don't see the problem," Cu grumbled, leaning against a tree and making it groan in protest.

Mave shoved past Cu, jarring him in the hip and making him snarl. "I invited Rhiannon because she is of the Otherworld. We shouldn't have much issue passing through the Ninth Wave with her aid. And Morrigan will be useful against the Fomori."

"Splendid. It sounds like we have *half* a plan. Let's head to Patrick's place and flesh it out," Erimon announced.

"Patrick? The leprechaun?" Morrigan asked, arching a thin, dark brow.

Mave tapped her nail against her sword's hilt. "But the Chaun isn't home."

"That has never stopped us before, my dear Mave," Erimon added. "Everyone touch so I can port us in one go. Come on. Time is of the essence."

"Oh, no. I only travel one way. I'll meet you all there." Morrigan swirled an arm around herself, shifting to the inky flock of crows, and ascended to the skies.

Finn grumbled before sliding a large hand over Mave's shoulder. I stroked Emrys' crest to soothe him for what was about to happen. Everyone followed suit, and Erimon took us to Patrick's house in Ireland. It seemed like only yesterday we were in Patrick's kitchen when Phoebe decided she'd marry him so he could remain on the surface and help fight the Dullahan—to help *me*.

Finn darted for the woods, the sounds of him hurling up his lunch echoing off the trees. Erimon raised his hand to the door, dissolving it into wood shards and allowing us entry. He stepped from the open doorway, gesturing everyone to move inside. I was the last, but he halted me by sliding a finger down the back of my stretchy pants and gently pulling me backward. He took the raven from my shoulder, coaxing him to fly inside the house. After spotting several bread rolls in a wooden bowl on the kitchen table, the bird obliged.

"You all start talking things over. Abby and I have a few matters to attend to before we join ye," Erimon said, returning the door to its full wooden strength before any of them could say a word.

Matters to attend to. I knew Erimon probably meant training me with my new power, but a larger part of me hoped he meant he planned to fuck me senseless in the middle of the forest. My insides twisted from the dirty thoughts circling my brain.

"Come now, Abby," Erimon whispered, interlacing his fingers with mine and brushing his lips across my brow. "Training first, and if you're a good girl, *then* I'll fuck you senseless."

My face warmed.

"How did you—" Pressing my palm against his chest, I coaxed him back so I could see his face. "—I didn't project that to you."

Erimon, using the hand intertwined with mine, scratched his neck. "You didn't?"

Slowly, I shook my head.

"Huh. I don't know whether to be excited or horrified at the prospect of being able to read each other's minds at will."

I yanked him forward, rising to the balls of my feet to suck on his bottom lip before giving it a nip. "Horrified, why? That I'd be able to hear all your naughty, scandalous thoughts?"

"No," he replied, gruff and husky. "Those I'll give ye freely." Erimon slapped my ass and led me toward the trees. "We've got a lot of ground to cover in a short amount of time. I'm praying you're a quick learner."

With science? With house cleaning hacks? Building a computer? Sure. I could learn anything I put my mind to relatively quickly, but wielding fiery Druid magic? That was an entirely new concept. And one, despite everything and everyone around me, I still, at moments, had a hard time wrapping my brain around.

Erimon found a vast clearing free of plant life so I wouldn't accidentally ignite some and start a forest fire. He squeezed my hands before taking several steps back and folding his hands in front of him. "Now, show me what you got, Bandruí."

8

ABBY

SEVERAL MINUTES PASSED, AND I stood with my palms aimed at the sky and stared at my hands doing nothing but simply existing. My power went haywire in my tiny apartment, but now, with Erimon watching and space to let loose, it went dormant. Figures.

Blowing out a frustrated breath, I dropped my hands at my sides. "I don't know what's going on, Erimon."

"Relax," he said, soothing and patient. Erimon rubbed my arms and bumped a knuckle under my chin. "Probably just a bit of performance jitters with me watchin' you. Or maybe you're secretly worried about lighting my jacket on fire again?"

I gave an exaggerated shrug.

"Here." He patted my elbow before slipping the jacket off, revealing those tanned, muscular arms and his taut chest stretching the material of his white tank top. Erimon tossed the garment aside and held his arms out, making his biceps flex. "Better?"

Much better. But probably for reasons he wasn't intending.

Chewing on my lip, I nodded, my gaze fixed on his matching sleeve tattoo. My own ink tingled, tantalizing my skin at the sight of it, and my core tightened.

Erimon's hand slid over my cheek, beckoning my attention away from the perfection he called his torso. "Try again, Abby," he whispered, his thumb tracing my cheekbone. His glacially blue eyes caught the sunlight, sparkling as he backed away to give me space.

The sun blazed boldly and brightly above us without a cloud in sight. Inhaling a deep breath, I focused on its warmth and closed my eyes. Turning my palms up, I envisioned collecting the sun's power in my hands, willing it to grace me with a portion of its rays.

"You're doin' it, love," Erimon said, a twinge of pride resonating in his tone.

Fluttering my eyes open, I stilled. A fireball flickered in my right hand, not unruly or chaotic, just resting there, waiting for me to do something with it. "What do I do now?"

Erimon widened his stance and tightened his jaw. "Hurl it at me."

"What?" The flame brightened and doubled in size. "I don't want to hurt you."

The usual amusement was gone from Erimon's gaze. A fierce and stoic glint flashed in his eyes before he gestured to me now. "You won't. Now throw it at me like I'm the Dullahan, and I'm here to *collect.*"

Memories of that day I lay dying in Erimon's arms went erratic through my mind like a video collage on fast forward.

The tip of the spine whip lodging in my chest, the pressure of it at first, and then pain when the Dullahan tore it out. Phoebe's wails of sorrow. Finn attempting to heal me but I'd been too far gone. Erimon speaking in Gaelic repeating the word *beo* over and over, like a plea to Mother Nature.

Using the fury that had built, my tattoo glowing in radiant crimson, I hurled the fire at Erimon. He fanned his palm, deflecting it with a small surging splash of water from the brook behind him. The fire was extinguished, and nothing burnt to the ground. The restlessness that had been growing, itching at my skin, felt more satisfied but still crawled at the surface of my mind, my soul, my gut.

"Good," Erimon said with a firm nod. "Now again, but conjure it faster and react as *soon* as you have it in your palm. Let me show you."

Erimon crouched to one knee, pressing his fingertips against the ground but keeping eye contact with me. The dirt vibrated beneath my feet, and several stones and pebbles floated toward Erimon, hovering near him. Erimon flicked his other hand in the same breath, and the rocks flew at me, but not one hit—they *bordered* me.

"How do you have so much control?" I still hadn't blinked, and I stared at him wide-eyed.

Erimon stood tall and dusted his hands. "Many, many years of practice. You'll get there. The most important thing right now is to know, without hesitation, when you want a fireball, it'll be there. Because that one instant you let your mind falter could very well be life or death, Abby." His lips slid downward, a concerned cinch forming between his brows.

A fierce determination tugged at my bones—the will to survive. I flew my hand open, immediately willing the fire to appear in my palm. It didn't happen immediately; it took several seconds, but it was the fastest I'd been able to command it thus far. I kept repeating this action over and over until seconds turned into milliseconds, and after an hour of attempting, it finally happened the instant I conjured it.

"I'm exhausted, Erimon." I closed my hand to extinguish the flame and rubbed my temples. "And hungry."

Erimon looped his arm with mine, leading me to several bushes under a canopy of trees with vibrant green leaves. "It's probably good to take a break anyway. Because that'll tell us if you can do what you just did again and again, without fail. To see if your body is puttin' it to memory."

"What are you feeling when you know it's going to obey you?" There were dozens of berries on each of the bushes, and I trailed my fingertips over them, sensing if they were riddled with poison. Once satisfied, I began plucking and shoving the sweet red berries into my mouth like a starving squirrel.

Erimon pressed a finger to the point on my spine where my neck met my back. "A tingle right here."

His touch sent shockwaves of pleasurable static coursing over my skin and swirling in my belly. Turning to face him, I lifted some of the berries, offering to feed him. Erimon squinted before parting his lips for me, allowing me to slide some past his lips. The tip of his tongue grazed my finger, and the tingling sensations surged through me now, our tattoos pulsing.

Our gazes fused together, unfaltering and heated. Taking those same fingers, I slid them into my mouth, tasting the mixture of him and the berries—sweet and earthy. A throttling pulse surged between my thighs, and it was as if I couldn't help myself that the need to have him, to devour him, far surpassed any rational thought attempting to take over.

"Abby," Erimon said through a strangled breath. He rested his hands on my shoulders, not on the sides to knead them as he had before. He pinched his eyes shut as if anguished before blasting them open again. "I want to say fuck it all and be with you just as badly, *luachmhar*."

Luachmar.

Why had the word seemed so familiar but so far away from my understanding?

"But? It sounded like there was a but in there, Druid." I bunched the front of his tank top tightly in my grasp, knowing what he was about to say but not wishing to hear it.

"We must have you ready. We'll have all the time in the world in the most literal sense to have each other from every angle and every surface once this is all settled." Erimon's hand curled the back of my neck and he pressed a light kiss to my forehead.

Have each other.

This warrior, this man of myth, has positively ruined me in the most poetic way.

"Then I've had enough rest. The sooner I get a handle on my power, the sooner we can go after the Dullahan and put a stop to all of this." Reluctantly, I backed away from him, swirling my hands around each other, fire forming within.

Erimon arched his brow, watching the tendrils of sunlight encircle the fiery orb like a charged star—fire forged from the sun itself, a miniature form of it, floated on my palm. Once I could feel its full power against my skin, knowing if I pulled any more, it could explode in my face, that sizzling sensation at the base of my spine roused me to action, and I launched it at Erimon.

Erimon's jaw tightened before he curled his hands in time to catch the fireball, a piece of it lashing his arm, burning it. He hissed and squelched the raging fire with dirt pulled from beneath his boots.

"Erimon," I started, stepping forward in a panic that I'd *harmed* him.

Erimon held a finger up, halting me, and shook his head. "You're fine, Abby. You can't hurt me. And what you just did? *That* is precisely what we need you to do."

The skin on my hands burned, but not in a painful way. I gazed at my palms, each line and groove that made up my unique print still glowed with orange embers.

"Again, *luachmhar.* Repeat it until you can hardly stand to lift your hands. Because we need your mind to know what to do when you command it." Erimon widened his stance, his arms raised and ready for whatever I might toss his way next.

And I did as he asked, willing the petite fireballs in my hands on repeat, hurling them at Erimon, only to do it again a breath later once he extinguished them. By the seventh time conjuring my power, I became distracted. Frantic memories of almost being eaten alive by a kelpie, nearly losing Phoebe from the venom of a hell spawn canine's bite. And the heat scorching my skin and suffocating me in that damn box with Erimon doing anything he could to keep me awake.

The fireball had started to form but sputtered and fizzled

into nothingness. Erimon sprung his falcon wings, zooming toward me with the speed of a—galloping horse. A sword formed in his palm within seconds, using the surrounding ore provided, and the blade hovered at my throat.

"One. Instant," he announced, but his eyes blazed when he caught sight of what I was doing.

The instinct came to me like a breath into my lungs. As much as both metal and the sun were part of nature, metal could *melt*. I'd pressed my hand to the blade, my fingertips blazing orange like a raging hearth within a forge. It didn't take long for the blade to take on the same intensity, and drips of iron fell to the ground, hardening.

"How in the dubnos did you know how to do that?" Erimon stood with his hand raised as if a sword rested there. He stared at me bewildered and then lowered his gaze to the dirt.

Turning my hands to peer at my knuckles, I shook my head. "I don't know. It just came to me. All of this is moving so fast, maybe I should—"

Erimon's mouth pressed to mine, his hands clasping the back of my neck and his thumbs resting at the corners of my jaw. He kissed me—deeply, erotically, and utterly feral. At first, I'd been taken aback, but I wrapped my arms around his neck, pressing my chest against his. He slid one hand to my ass and hoisted me, encouraging me to curl his waist with my legs.

A dozen flapping wings fluttered in the sky above us, and I paid it no mind until a familiar voice echoed in my skull.

"I see practice is going well," Morrigan said.

Erimon hissed, still holding onto me, but spun on his heel to look at her. "Elder's ass, Mor. What are you doing here?

You're supposed to be at Patrick's place."

Morrigan leaned on a tree, absently flicking something from her black fingernail. "I know, but I figured I'd spend the least amount of time around Rhiannon and the Hound as possible. Besides—" Her lips took a wicked curve upward. "—this is far more entertaining."

Erimon let me slide down his body until my feet met the ground. His hardness pressed against my core as I went, and the memory of how it felt inside me had me pinching my thighs together. "As if we're goin' to continue in front of you."

Morrigan pouted and pretended to kick a pebble. "Why not? Don't let my petty little presence ruin what needs to be done at some point anyway."

Me and Erimon arched brows at her.

"What needs to be done?" I asked.

Erimon flicked his wrist at her as if her words held no meaning. With what little I knew about Morrigan, it was apparent that her words meant *everything*.

9

ERIMON

BLEEDIN' PIXIES. I WON'T DENY Morrigan will be extremely helpful in the battle to come, but her presence always brings delight or darkness. Sometimes both, but more often one, or the other. Considering that she's determined to stay on my coattails and has a growing interest in Abby, it put me on edge. And Abby didn't need something else to worry about. The Dullahan and Balor were more than enough, especially when she grappled with her mortality and newborn Druid power.

Pulling a wood splinter from a nearby tree, I used it as a pick and stuck it between my teeth. "No riddles, Mor. Come out with it."

Morrigan sighed like I'd ruined all her fun. "You two are bonded. And with that comes the needed art of *mating*."

"I'm sorry?" Abby coughed, her cheeks turning crimson.

It wasn't news to me. I'd already known what the never-ending twitch in my cock was from and the dull ache in my stomach that was like a constantly clenched muscle with only one way to relax it. But this ritual wouldn't disappear much like it hadn't after the first time we'd fucked after bonding. It would grow in intensity each time. It would eat at us like an insufferable gnat and after the ceremony with the Elder? I reckoned it'd start to consume us, which was why I'd remained silent about it because having sex, as much as I wanted to do nothing more than that, should be very low on the priority list.

And then here came Morrigan, the Phantom Queen, to throw it all to shit.

"Has he not told you?" Morrigan's eyes brightened, and the mischievous smile that rivaled a shot fox had me reeling.

"Mor," I growled.

Abby's eyes turned into slits aimed at me. I snatched the pick from my mouth and held up a finger. "I've got a grand explanation, love."

Morrigan, looking rather pleased with herself, sat on a stump and crossed her legs. Give her a damn bag of popcorn, and she'd be gearing up to be entertained.

"Erimon?" Abby turned to me, her expression far from the angered one I'd expected. She chewed on her bottom lip, and a wrinkle formed in the skin between her caramel eyes.

Ignoring Morrigan's constant grinning, I took Abby's hands in mine and rubbed between her knuckles with my thumbs. "When two beings are bonded as we are, the connection requires consistent—"

"Mating," Morrigan cut in.

After tossing her a seething glare, I offered a warm smile to Abby. "I'm not a fan of usin' that word because it takes all of the luster out of it, but yes."

A recognizable heat stirred in my Abby's eyes. Her throat bobbed, and my gaze darted straight to it. Her lips parted, and it took everything in me not to say fuck it, that Morrigan was meters away, shove Abby's chest against a tree, yank down those skin-tight pants, and screw her senseless.

"The full moon isn't going to wait for us to be ritualistic." I winced at my bulge straining against my pants, hard as fuckin' granite.

Morrigan let out a frustrated groan and moved between us. "And you two aren't going to be much help if you're thoroughly distracted. Fine. Don't do it now. But for the betterment of the team and her *life*, Erimon. It has to happen before we fight the Dullahan. However, you want to go about it, however quick you want to make it, see that it's done, hm?" She flicked some midnight hair from her eyes and mumbled, "Stars, I never thought I'd have to *convince* two people to have sex."

I played with the ring on my forefinger. "I heard that."

"It's true." Morrigan gestured at Abby. "She's gorgeous. And you're—not bad on the eyes. It shouldn't be this difficult."

Ignoring Morrigan and the come-hither eyes Abby gave me, I turned away and rubbed my neck. "We should get back to the rest of them. We'll keep training there, but I can't trust those four to plan this entirely on their own."

"I'll meet you there." Black, inky tendrils swirled Morrigan's body. "But remember what I said, Druid." The black smoke engulfed her until she transformed into a flock of crows and flew away.

Abby chewed on her thumbnail and folded her arms over her stomach, unable to make eye contact with me.

Sucking in a breath, I thought about the sight of Finn naked, hoping it'd calm down my very eager dick, before stepping to Abby's side. "You alright?"

She nodded, but still wouldn't look at me.

"Abby," I beckoned, resting a hand on her shoulder. She melted at my touch, nuzzling her cheek against my knuckles. A shaky breath escaped her parted lips, and she turned to face me. "We'll get through this."

Her eyes grew heavy, and she walked her fingers up my stomach. "*Having* me is a chore now, Druid?"

Grimacing but not wanting her to stop, I pinched my thigh with my free hand. "Not having you and saying to fuck with the plan is the chore here, love."

Abby let her hand fall flat at her side with a defeated sigh that wrenched my heart, stomach, and groin. "Let's hatch out this plan then."

Not trusting myself in this forest any longer, I ported us to Patrick's house. Morrigan stood outside, lurking by a window, idly chuckling to herself. Shouting came from inside, one voice belonging to a male, the other a female.

"I was wrong. This is far more entertaining," Morrigan said, snorting.

"Shite," I grumbled, sprinting inside with Abby hot on my heels.

Cu and Mave stood at opposite sides of the table, their chairs on the floor behind them like they'd both stood up with fury. Finn sat between them like a moderator but kept silent, his arms folded, his expression bored and irritated. Rhiannon remained in the corner with her unicorn, calmly stroking its muzzle.

Cu pointed at Mave. "How do you plan to do that when we haven't solved the Ninth Wave problem?"

"For the tenth time, Hound, we have. It's her," Mave retorted, gesturing to Rhiannon behind her.

"Oh, right. The one who hasn't said a damn word this entire time we've been debating. How can we trust her?" Cu slammed his palms to the table, making the mugs and plate of mixed fruit on it bounce.

"Pipe down, the lot of ye," I roared, glaring between my fellow ethereal beings and shaking my head. "I leave you all to do one job and come back to nothing but your usual bickerin'?"

Mave pushed from the table. "He started it."

"Real mature, *Queen* Mave," Cu snapped back.

Morrigan sauntered past me, holding up the nearest wall by casually leaning on it, that same serpentine grin snaking over her lips.

"You two, sit down, and shut up for a moment," I ordered, then looked at Rhiannon. "You, we need to hear how you plan to get us past the Ninth Wave and for Elder's sake, *why* is the unicorn inside the house?"

Abby's heat tantalized my skin, followed by her slender fingers grasping my bicep.

You're even more attractive when you get into boss mode.

A tingle swirled down my spine, landing at my tailbone and shooting straight into the base of my cock.

I'll put that to memory.

I'd thought the words back to her, eliciting an alluring smile that had me rocking on my heels. Shaking the numerous scandalous thoughts having a party in my mind, I forced my attention back to Rhiannon.

"Surely you don't expect me to keep my faithful companion outside in the elements? She's far too majestic for such a filthy place." Rhiannon kissed the creature's single horn.

Looking around at the dirt-covered wooden floorboards, the several layers of dust adorning various items, and the cobwebs strung from the light fixtures, I raised a brow at her. "I believe outside is far less dirty than in here, but at any rate, so long as the animal doesn't shit on the floor, you can keep her inside if it means you'll plan with us."

Rhiannon bowed her head, and we moved to the round table with the others, surrounding it like King Arthur's knights.

"Do you know where the Elder is, Mor?" There was no beating around this particular bush any longer. Before any of this would work, Abby needed to be immortal and eternally bound to me.

Morrigan propped her feet on the table, toes sticking out from a midnight black pair of stiletto heels with a snake-wrap swirling up her ankles. "I do."

The room fell silent.

Morrigan snatched an apple from the fruit bowl and took a bite, not elaborating.

I leaned on the table and beat my index finger on it. "Care to enlighten us?"

"The Hill of Tara," Morrigan responded, grinning and taking another bite.

"Hold on." I paused, rubbing the bridge of my nose. "You're telling me he's been in Ireland this entire time? And there, of all places?"

Finn hooted with laughter until I seethed at him. He abruptly stopped but pulled his lips into his mouth as if he struggled not to continue.

Mave also stifled a chuckle. "Wasn't that where High Kings used to *frolic* about?" Despite her best efforts, she snorted.

Mave got an extra cold steely glare from me, and she made a gesture of zipping her mouth shut, but mirth still danced rebelliously in her eyes.

"You *do* still need the Lia Fáil to allow you entry. I'd suggest Abby touch it and not you. Wouldn't want to risk the Elder digging up old hatchets," Morrigan said, amusement dancing in her violet gaze.

Furiously raking a hand through my hair, I blew out a harsh breath. "Fine. The first part is settled, and the next, we barter a ship again and make it to the Ninth Wave whilst battling Fomori. Then?" I turned my attention to Rhiannon.

"You appeal to Clíodhna," Rhiannon responded with such confidence and simplicity as if any of us knew how to do this.

Mave propped on one elbow. "The Banshee Queen?"

"Yes." Rhiannon nodded. "She rules the Ninth Wave now and controls how calm or catastrophic it will be. Appeal to her desires, and she'll let us pass without consequence."

"And how do we do that? Compliment her looks?" Finn asked, tracing a hand over his beard.

"Her desires are never the same. With me in your company will grant her favor, but we need to give her a gift if we want to pass without confrontation." Rhiannon sat on the edge of the table and rested her hands on her lap.

"Sounds like a lot of useless work when we could just be—"

Morrigan had removed a dagger from her belt and used it to pick her fingernails. "—confrontational."

"Put away the claws, Mor. We're already going to have enough on our plate to fight and will take any opportunity to avoid it when we can," I ordered.

Rhiannon lifted her chin at Morrigan, who stabbed her knife into the table, making Rhiannon jump.

"There's still the tiny matter of the Dullahan and luring him *and* Balor to the Otherworld with us," Mave added, sinking in her chair enough to rest her head on the back of it.

"Is she even ready for this?" Cu asked, his gaze fixed on Abby.

On cue, Abby sparked a fiery orb in her palm, eyes glued to Cu as she did it. Once fully formed, she flicked her wrist and sent it catapulting toward him. Cu's eyes widened like full moons, and he lifted his gauntlet to block it.

"Are you mad?" Cu roared, rising to his feet.

The power that bubbled in my Abby's veins. And how quickly she's been latching onto it. There was no stopping the insatiable lust surging through me like a lightning strike now. Abby's tattoo still glowed red, and she locked her gaze on me from across the room. A sultry smile tugged at her lips, and desperation played in her eyes.

I need you.

That dull ache pulsed in my stomach, borderline painful now, and I resisted the urge to adjust the growing bulge in my trousers.

"Um, maybe we should all leave," Finn said.

They stared at us.

"Or not," Morrigan added.

Shaking my head, I crossed the room to my awaiting Bandruí, my heart thundering in my chest, threatening to punch a hole in it. "No need. We're going to the woods."

Abby's face melted into exhilaration—anticipation of what was about to happen. If the others said anything behind us, I didn't hear them because my focus lay solely on Abby's quickening breaths and her erratic pulse that matched mine. I hoisted her over my shoulder with her ass to the sky. After splintering the door and melding it back together as soon as my boots crossed the threshold, I made for the forest with my bonded Druid on my shoulder and a frenzy I couldn't ignore any longer.

10

ABBY

AN IDEA OR THOUGHT THAT continually preoccupies or intrudes on a person's mind—an obsession. That's what I'd felt for Erimon since he gave some of himself to me. It started subtly at first, but within a breath's reach of him again over the last few days, it has blossomed into a growing *imperative* desire.

When Erimon slid me from his shoulder to rest my feet on the ground, I clutched his shirt and tilted my chin at him. "Take us to the Bog Garden."

A fire flickered in Erimon's gaze, and his palm pressed tighter against my lower back, bringing me closer.

The Bog Garden was the first place we'd made love—a mystical faerie woodland that I'd missed ever since. It had become our refuge—our escape from the known world to a forest sanctuary. Now, it called me back to it.

Erimon nuzzled his cheek against the side of my head. "You don't need me to go there now, Abby. Why don't *you* take us there?"

Frowning, I played my fingers up and down his neck. "I don't know how."

"Yes, you do." Gently, Erimon began to sway us back and forth like a calming waltz. "It's no different than willing the fire into your palm and casting it in a given direction."

Letting my eyes fall shut, I channeled my power, its essence thrumming beneath my skin, edging toward the surface. I slid my hand up Erimon's stomach, landing on his chest, and a sudden pulse pushed from my fingertips. A breath later, my hair swaying behind me, sounds of bubbling brooks and tiny pairs of faerie wings beating blessed my ears.

"You always were so impatient, *luachmhar*," Erimon said through a raspy chuckle.

The faintest scent of something burning hit my nostrils no sooner had he said it, and I blazed my eyes open only to be greeted by a *very* shirtless Druid. What remained of his shirt lay in embers, and cloth pieces singed at the edges near his booted feet.

As my gaze roamed his chiseled torso, traveling until I landed on his matching tattoo, a moan bubbled in my throat, *aching* for him. "I still don't have a full handle on my powers." Guilt tried to creep its way in, but Erimon's half-naked form, mixed with his intoxicating scent of earth and pine, made my mind hazy.

"And it's not going to be." Erimon edged closer, trailing his touch over my tattoo, still glowing fiery crimson, his own reacting in shimmering swirls of cerulean dust. "It doesn't have to be perfect to defeat the Dullahan. Only reliable."

Wicked thoughts consumed my entire being, and I coaxed

Erimon backward—past the dewy willow trees, the trailing bunches of colorful flowers, and the curious fluttering faeries. "Then let me practice—" We reached the mossy knoll Erimon created for us the last time, and I gave him a light push until a devilish grin curved his lips, realizing my intent, and he sank to lay against it. "—on you."

"Then use me as you see fit, Bandruí." Erimon's gaze became hooded as he undid the button on his jeans, making the effort of unzipping torturously slow, tantalizing me.

Following his pace, I inched my shirt off first, followed by everything else, until I stood naked and free. Erimon blew out a breath once he took me all in as if it were the first time he saw me like this. But things *were* so different between us now. It felt fresh and vibrant.

I sank to my knees, crawling across the mossy threshold to my awaiting warrior Druid. Prowling over him like a nymph in heat, I dragged my breasts across his stomach, trailing his chest, and stopped right below his mouth. He bucked beneath me, his hardness brushing that sensitive spot, and making my breath hitch. Erimon nipped at one of my nipples, flicking his tongue over it, but that was all I let him do for now. Because I couldn't wait any longer, the need for him inside me grew into a painful surge in my core.

Positioning over him, straddling his hips, I lowered myself, my head rolling back as bit by bit of him filled me to the hilt. The sensual connection lit my tattoo, blazing crimson sparkling tendrils. Erimon's ink shone in shimmers of spiraling sapphire, and the two colors swirled together, creating overlapping purple streaks. I paused there, my insides throbbing around him, his length pulsing.

"Fuck," Erimon moaned in a drawn-out hissing snarl. His neck craned backward, his fingers kneading into my hip bones.

"I want to see your wings, Erimon," I asked, bordering on begging.

A snarky smile played over his lips before he obliged me, and the falcon wings flared out. The feathers rustled and stretched before nestling in place once Erimon settled into it. I chewed on my lip, reaching for the apex of one wing, delicately trailing my touch over it.

Erimon's eyes pinched shut, and he sucked in a breath. "That's fuckin' new."

Storing that in my brain for later, I moved my hand from his wings. Slowly, blissfully, and torturously slow, I rocked against him, arching my back with every thrust, and already shuddering at the merge of sensations skyrocketing through me. I bunched my hair with one hand, the other trailing down my face, one finger catching on my lip. I no longer thought in words or rational sentences, only with tree whispers and the earth's thrums of life. Erimon's heartbeat, our steady intune breaths, and the whistling of the wind through the forest canopy were the only sounds I cared to hear. Erimon tensed beneath me, his heels digging into the ground, his grip tightening on my waist.

Fluttering my eyes open, I was blessed with the sight of Erimon fighting his release too soon. His face grimaced, and he let out the sexiest, most masculine, frustrated growl I'd ever heard. When his shoulders relaxed and his hands loosened, only then did I start to move again. The euphoria built in my center, whirling through my stomach until it erupted in static and that tightening pressure released. I cried out through the pleasuring tremors, my legs shaking. The fire magic bestowed to me roared in my veins, glowing and crackling. Collapsing to Erimon's chest, I pressed a hand to his sternum, practicing on him as he asked.

Erimon hissed, not in pain, but in arousal. I willed the same warming sensations tantalizing my skin to surge through him in tandem. Our veins glowed with equaling orange embers, pulsing to the mirrored rhythm of our erratic heartbeats.

"Very impressive, Bandruí," Erimon whispered hoarsely before sitting up, wrapping my legs around his waist. "But I've yet to *claim* you."

The word alone made my clit tense in response.

Erimon snaked a hand to the back of my head, pulling my mouth to his and thrusting his tongue past my lips, swirling with mine. Desperate for friction, I started to rock against him, but his free hand held me still. He grinned wickedly against my lips, pulling away, and shaking his head. Those glacial eyes sparked with mirth, and in the next instance, he had me on my hands and knees, palms pressed into the highest point of the slanted mossy rock.

Grey clouds formed in the sky now, the low rumblings of thunder barely audible in the difference. Scents of an impending rainstorm permeated the air around us, and I encouraged Mother Nature to unleash it all on us. Because a torrential downpour was me right now, at this moment—all-consuming, powerful, and soaking *wet.*

He tilted my hips skyward, making me present more of

myself to him. Delicately, he dragged a finger between my folds, groaning at how deliciously wet I was still for him. I gasped when his moist tongue lapped over me, repeatedly stroking and flicking, *tasting* my arousal. My nails dug into the emerald moss, ripping some of it from the stone.

When his mouth tore away from me, I stifled a whimper, already missing his sensual, wicked kiss. Thunder boomed above us now, lightning strikes sizzling through the darkness. Erimon walked his fingers up my spine, sending tiny electric pulses through my skin with each passing touch.

"Oh, my—" I said through a moan, my words escaping me.

Between the blend of my fire and Erimon's lightning, blessed by the storm brewing in the sky, my insides were a blissful, electric, raging inferno, and I wanted more—*needed* more.

"Erimon," I groaned, flashing a sultry gaze at him over my shoulder.

He didn't answer me, only grabbed each of my hips and slammed into me, taking me from behind. My back arched, my head throwing back, and Erimon caught my hair within his grasp, his other hand moving to my shoulder. With every pound, every thrust and pump, the storm grew in intensity— thunder rattled the trees, vibrated the ground, and the lightning shone so bright in the sky that it illuminated jagged patterns around us.

Erimon let go of my hair and lifted me high enough for his teeth to find my nape, where he lightly bit me, an animalistic snarl bubbling in the back of his throat. "I *need* to be bonded to you, Abby. I don't know how much longer I can physically stand it."

"I know," I replied in a breathy whisper.

And I did know. Even as we joined, it still didn't feel like enough. Even as he made love to me in the present moment, claimed me, *mated* with me. My mind deemed it inadequate for what we were to each other. Unlike what I'd felt with him before, a tingling sensation, settled in the back of my skull, and the next breath I took filled not only my lungs but my very being. My senses went into overdrive—the moss at my palm felt softer, the wind rustling the leaves sounded clearer, and the overlapping scents of dirt and impending rain—Erimon's scent, *my* scent, were enough to consume me.

His thrusts quickened, his hips slamming against my ass, and I clenched around him. Rain fell in a watery curtain over us, drenching our bodies almost instantaneously. It was fresh and earthy, and all of it sent me over the edge. Erimon pumped several more times before stilling, roaring into the downpour falling in droves around us, jerking through his own release, his one hand delicately gripping my chin, the other holding on for dear life at my hip.

Our tattoos still glowed in vibrant shades of ruby and azure, the rain misting against them, turning them neon. Erimon didn't pull out of me straight away. Instead, he lifted me so my back pressed to his chest and kissed the shell of my ear.

Sputtering and blinking away the raindrops from his eyelashes, he sighed against my skin. "I will never be apart from you like that ever again, *luachmhar*. That's a promise."

"Quite the promise, Druid." I reached behind me, finding the back of his head, and dragging my nails across his scalp. "How do you plan to keep it?"

Wind gusts played through my wet hair and fluttered over my nipples, making them hard as granite. I whimpered and nuzzled against him, knowing full well it was Erimon's doing.

"By never leaving your side. And if we have to be apart for whatever reason, I pray our official bonding will only strengthen our unseen communication." Erimon trailed the breeze down my back, giving me goosebumps. "But we'll be an unstoppable force whether we're around one another or not. Protecting each *other*."

When I turned to face him, Erimon slowly pulled out of me and splayed his arms to wrap them around me, hugging my head to his chest. "We have to get back. Morrigan knows where the Elder is, and if the bond gives us clarity, we're going to need it for this battle."

Erimon smiled into my hair. "This battle. Listen to you. Already a warrior."

The word had come so naturally I didn't realize I'd said it.

Leaning back, I searched Erimon's expression. "You're stalling. Are you afr—"

Erimon's finger pressed to my lips. "It's not fear so much as it is concern that he won't be willing to perform the ritual because it's for *me*."

"But you've changed so much. Surely, he'll recognize that?" I nestled my cheek against his palm that still hovered near my face.

Erimon let out a deep sigh and absently traced patterns in my tattoo. "With how long we Druids live, centuries' worth of behavior normally takes double the time to get over it."

"Maybe you're not giving him enough credit. You called the punishment he gave you a curse, but is that what I am to you?

A burden?" An ache settled over my chest despite knowing Erimon didn't think that.

His gaze snapped to mine, and he pulled me closer by seizing my shoulders. "No. Abby Weber, you are the opposite of a curse. You're an antidote, a blessing. You are *luck* personified."

My heart rocketed to the skies, waltzing with the stars before settling in my chest. "Then maybe you've been viewing it wrong this entire time, Erimon. Because it sounds like the Elder gave you the path you would've never taken on your own." I took his face in my hands, swirling my thumbs over his high cheekbones. "He wanted to ensure you met *me*."

Erimon's gaze brightened, his jaw twitching before an enchanting, sparkling grin tugged at his lips. "It seems you truly are an enchantress."

Rolling my eyes, but feeling my cheeks warm all the same, I swatted his shoulder. "Where do you come from, Erimon?"

Erimon's face contorted as if entirely put off by what I thought to be a simple question. "Ancient—Ireland? Born into royalty. Raised a Druid."

Stifling a laugh, I shook my head and cupped his chin with one hand. "No. I know all that. Where do you come from? Who were you before all this warrior Druid business? You have to have been a child at some point, right? Scraping your knees on rocks when you were too careless running amuck in the woods?"

A forlorn smile appeared across Erimon's lips, and he took one of my hands, interlacing our fingers. "I'm afraid there's not many stories like that to tell. With the family I hail from and the making of a Druid coursing my veins, I started training magically, strategically, and politically no sooner had I begun to speak."

My heart seized in my chest. "That's awful. You never got to just be a kid?"

"As an infant, perhaps?" Erimon traced over my knuckles like peaks and valleys. "The earliest memory I have of bein' somewhat mortal was my older brother teaching me how to make a rocking horse out of wood." Erimon's jaw tightened, and I squeezed his hand, knowing that remembering his brother, having killed him in war centuries ago, was painful.

"Did you use it afterward?" I offered a half-smile, envisioning a tiny Erimon rocking back and forth on a wooden horse with a radiant smile.

Erimon nodded and chuckled. "Every damn day until my da tore me off it and said it'd be the last time I played for fun. That it was time to become a man."

A fist-sized lump formed in my throat, and I tugged Erimon's arm, urging him to look at me. "You've become a warrior Druid whose loyalty to his people stretches far beyond any *man* I've known. I'm sorry you didn't get to live before being thrust into this entire world."

"I came to grips with it long, long ago, love. But what about you? I remember you mentioning being a foster care child. Did you wind up in a home to at least grow up in the end?" Erimon tilted his head to one side, genuine concern sparking in his gaze.

I hated thinking about this part of my life. But if I was to spend an eternity with this Druid, he deserved to know all there was about me.

"Eventually, yes. But it was only for the time I was in high school, and the house had seven other teenagers in it." Raking a hand through my hair, I sniffed once, pushing the pity for myself to the back of my mind. "I still think the couple did it for the tax break to this day. But I never knew what it felt like to be nurtured by a parent. And once each of us turned eighteen, it was time to go out on our own, get a job, live on the streets if we couldn't afford an apartment, but our time in that foster home would come to an abrupt end." Catching Erimon's knowing gaze, I softly nodded. "Ethereal or normal. Our childhoods were roughly the same."

Erimon's jaw set, and he leaned in, kissing me with a sort of newly discovered affection. "We need to find the Elder. Now," he commanded, scooping me into his arms and lifting a finger like he intended to port.

Grabbing his hand, I referenced our naked bodies. "Maybe some clothes first?"

"Right. Though I suppose I'll be showin' up shirtless, seeing as my woman has a fiery impatience," Erimon said, snickering and putting me down for me to get dressed.

My woman.

Smiling, I shimmied into my pants and threw the shirt over my head. "You drag it out of me." The fire flickered over my knuckles and, briefly, even danced in my gaze.

Erimon stood mesmerized by the light show before cradling me in his arms again. "I'm looking forward to what the future holds for us, Bandruí."

A meek smile crested my lips because the idea of losing him or him losing me tore my insides to shreds. Pushing the thought away, I kissed him, tangling my fingers in his unruly hair before saying, "Me too. And if we're lucky, we'll have an eternity for adventures."

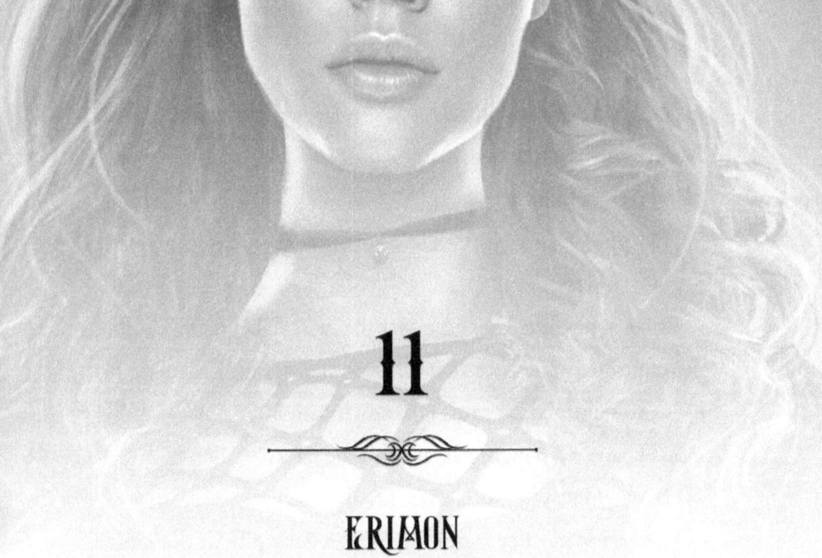

11

ERIMON

"LUCK," SHE SAID. IT WAS as if I wasn't already the luckiest son of a bollix on the godsforsaken planet that Abby Weber was *my* fated bond—a female Druid. The Elder was going to have a maniacal laugh at my expense once we found him, and I'd be a right fella taking it silently. At least, I hoped. Considering it'd been over a hundred years since making the wrinkly fart's company, I might have a lot more to get off my chest than I realized.

I ported us to Patrick's house with Abby still draped in my arms, only putting her down once I heard the most peculiar sounds coming from inside—nothing. It was quiet as a midnight cemetery in the dead of winter. Abby and I shared perplexed expressions before I stormed for the door, concern wrenching my spine.

I hurled the door open the old-fashioned way to find all five mystical heroes seated at the round table—playing *cards*. The unicorn stood at the window, warming its body on sun rays peeking through the blinds. No sooner had the raven spotted Abby, than it launched from Finn's shoulder straight to her outstretched hand.

"Do you have any sevens?" Finn asked, arching a bushy brow at Rhiannon.

Rhiannon panned her gaze over the cards in her hand, circling through them one by one with sloth-like speed. Cu rolled his eyes and slammed his cards face down with impatience, leaning in his chair and hanging an arm off the back.

"Nope. Go sink," Rhiannon finally said.

Finn nodded once, reaching for the deck pile in the table's center, but stopped short, eyeing Rhiannon quizzically.

"For the third time, Rhian, it's go *fish*," Mor spat, slamming her elbows on the table with about as equal irritation as Cu.

Rhiannon stacked her cards in a neat pile and placed them on the table in front of her, blinking her large eyes. "But why would you give your foe the opportunity to gain sustenance when you won the battle? Should we not wish for their misfortune instead?"

"See, Mor?" Mave waggled a finger at Rhiannon. "This is why we're friends."

After Finn took a card, he slipped it into his hand but paused, sniffing the air—once, twice, and the third time was an exceptionally deeper inhale.

"Please, don't let me, your dubious leader, keep you from recreation," I finally announced when none of them batted an eyelash at us.

With the raven perched on her shoulder, Abby moved closer to the table.

"Bleedin' dubnos," Finn barked, curling an arm over his nose and pushing from his seat. "It's *you*, Abby."

Abby frowned, nonchalantly sniffing near her armpits and shrugging. "What do you mean?"

Elder's arse. I knew I marked her but hadn't realized to what—extent. Now, if they could all politely let it drop, we could move on to more pressing matters.

"You positively reek of Druid, lass," Cu so eloquently announced.

Slapping a hand over my face, I let it slowly drag downward until it reached my beard.

Morrigan cackled and smacked the table several times as if cheering. "You wanted to be extra, *extra* sure, hm, Monny?"

I should've known this lot would never be able to keep their mouths shut about this.

"It's *us*, Erimon. Really think ye had to ward *us* away from your Druidly betrothed?" Finn pressed both giant hands to his chest, his nose still twitching over my scent lacing every one of Abby's curves, her skin, her *pores*.

Rhiannon lifted her chin, smelling the air and shrugging. "It's quite the pleasant scent if you ask me—piney, earthy, musky, and just a hint of something sweet."

"Druid," Abby beckoned, her tone undecipherable.

When I turned on my heel to look at her, her hands were on her hips, a dark brow arched, but fortunately, a pleasant smile also graced her lips. "Yes, my dear?"

"Care to explain what they're talking about?"

In front of the group? Not particularly.

Abby curled a finger in my pants and tugged me toward her.

"Try it, anyway."

How many times would I forget she could hear most of my thoughts before I caught on?

"During our—" pausing, I cleared my throat *loudly* "— escapades in the woods, I may have marked you as, well, mine. And perhaps I went a teensy bit more than I thought I had."

"Marked me?" Abby blanched before displaying the Dullahan's mark to me on the inside of her wrist. "Like this kind?"

Delicately taking her arm within my grasp, I pressed a kiss to my tattoo surrounding that damn mark. "Not at all. My mark is to let everyone, every*thing*, know that you're mine. Under my protection. And that I'll kill all I need to ensure you're safe."

Abby squinted at me with a clever grin. "Are you *jealous*?"

"Yes," Cu grumbled, grabbing the last apple from the bowl on the table.

After tossing Cu a seething glare, I turned back to Abby, taking her hands in mine. "I wouldn't go so far as to call it jealousy as I would my protective nature."

Abby nodded, contemplating something. "And can I— mark *you*?"

Of course not.

I opened my mouth to tell her just that, but Morrigan beat me to it.

"Yes. You can, Abby." Morrigan's smile said so much without elaboration, making my toes grip the insides of my boots.

"Can I, now?" Abby asked Morrigan but kept her playful gaze fixed on me. "Will you teach me?"

A breath pushed from my throat, and I choked on it.

"Absolutely," Morrigan answered.

Alright, Erimon, warrior Druid, this wasn't a big deal. So, you'll be marked by the only woman you could imagine spending eternity with. And anyone who came within a breath of you, male, female, or otherwise, would know you were hers and she yours.

After successfully having this mental conversation with myself with her hearing, I offered Abby a warm smile. "Only seems fitting we would both be jealous of anyone even thinkin' of stealing the other away."

Abby's cheeks turned rosy, and her mouth fell open. "I'm not jeal—" But I cut her off with a kiss, wrapping my arms around her and ignoring the moans and groans from the lads, whoops, and whistles from the ladies.

"I suppose you wish for attendance with the Elder now?" Morrigan asked as we pulled away from our embrace.

Abby licked her bottom lip, and I wanted nothing more than to suck it in my mouth and plunge my fingers inside her and—the frenzy had *just* been satisfied, and here it was starting all over again.

Grimacing, I shot my gaze to Morrigan and replied with a strained, "Yes. Unless, of course, you all wish to finish your little game first?"

"I wasn't playing much to begin with." Morrigan tossed her cards to the discarded pile and shot to her feet. "Meet me at the stone." A warm smile graced Morrigan's lips, aimed at Abby before she swirled into her flock of crows and flew out the window.

Just as I took Abby's hand in mine, the hovel door swung

open. At the entrance stood Phoebe and her leprechaun husband, who tried desperately to appear outraged.

"Erimon? I thought we agreed that my home wasn't to be used for our meetings any longer?" Patrick's nose twitched, and he folded his arms to attempt to make his shoulders wider.

Circling Abby's palm with my thumb, I sighed and dragged a hand through my hair. "Ah, yes, Patty, but that was months ago before we became a merry band of nine. You don't mind, right? It's temporary, after all."

Patrick blanched as he looked around the room. "I suppose it's not—" But when his gaze landed on the unicorn, his eyes bulged from his skull.

"We'll be right back," I announced, porting us to the awaiting Lia Fail stone and letting Finn simmer that particular boil down.

As the Lia Fail came to be known over time, The Stone of Destiny stood oblong and remote on a stony circular platform in the middle of rolling green meadows without a house or sign of civilization in sight. Long before my father was born, my ancestors used the stone to prove one's worthiness and allow passage to the Hills of Tara. But I never touched it. The life of a Druid was my calling, not some ceremonial right that served as more of a publicity stunt than anything of worth.

Morrigan leaned on the stone, squinting at the sun beating down on us. "Ever notice over the decades how it's come to look like a giant leaning cock?"

Abby tilted her head as if conjuring the imagery, and I huffed a coughing breath. "Elder's tongue, Mor. Don't call it that."

"Why?" Morrigan turned toward the erected stone and

pressed her cheek to it, her fingers idly stroking it. "Is it because you're going to have to *touch* it?"

The stone made no reaction to Morrigan, and it wouldn't because of who and what she was.

"What are you talking about? You said Abby should touch it." Pressing a hand to Abby's lower back, I coaxed her closer to me, yearning to feel her tattoo near my skin.

Morrigan pushed off the pillar with one finger, a devious grin tilting her lips. "Yes, but you have to as well, Druid. You are a package deal, are you not?"

Growling, I prowled toward the stone, leading Abby to it. "Go ahead, love. It won't bite."

"What am I supposed to feel? Or how is it supposed to react to me?" Abby's fingers hovered over the stone, staring at it, mesmerized.

Sidling behind her, I pressed a kiss to the back of her head and gently coaxed her hand forward until it rested on the stone. "Destiny, Abby."

And nothing happened. Morrigan was bleedin' right.

"Now you, Loverboy." Morrigan jutted her thumb at the stone.

I reached over Abby's shoulder and stopped short, my throat turning to sand and gravel.

"What's the matter?" Morrigan's face appeared in my peripheral vision. "Afraid of what it'll tell you?"

"Why would I be?" I asked through gritted teeth.

Morrigan combed Abby's hair with her fingers and sighed. "Because your destiny may not lie in the warrior way you hold so dear."

Shaking away Morrigan's infuriating words, I slapped my

palm to the stone. A burst of white light blazed around us, and the stone disappeared, along with Morrigan. We stood in more rolling emerald hills, but dozens of sheep grazed the grass, and smoke stacks from a quaint house's chimney fluttered the sky over one hill, a small wooden door situated at its base.

The Elder. He'd been so close, yet so far away this entire fucking time.

We stood several paces from the door, and I turned toward an antsy Abby, who was wringing her hands together and not blinking. Taking her fidgeting palms with my fingers, I gently squeezed. "Are you ready for this, Abby?"

"Yes. I'm just nervous. But I want this more than anything." Abby nodded with extra affirmation before squeezing my hands back. "Are you?"

It amazed me how I'd have found any excuse to port away from a situation like this hundreds of years ago—to cower to the shadows and leave it all behind. But not now. Not today. Not ever.

"For the first time in my life, Abigail Weber, I can honestly say with every fiber of my being—" Inching closer, I took her face in my hands and pressed a whispered kiss to her lips. "—yes."

She rubbed her nose against mine. "Then what are we waiting for?"

Yes. The sooner we went through this ritual, the sooner we could begin our immortal lives together. It didn't scare me, revolt me, *or* make me queasy as it once had.

Aye. Eternity awaits.

12

ABBY

FIREFLIES DANCED CIRCLES IN MY stomach. I wasn't nervous about spending the rest of my Druid life with Erimon, nor was I anxious about going through the ritual, yet my limbs still shook like autumn leaves in the wind. What would it feel like? How would things change? As Morrigan claimed, would my Bandruí side evolve into something beyond anything I could imagine?

Pushing it all aside, I curled my arm with Erimon's. Not waiting for him, I knocked on the wooden hovel door and stared at the intricate Celtic knot designs carved into it to distract myself. A few beats later, the door swung open, with nothing but scents of pine, myrrh, and something savory greeting us.

"I was beginning to think you wouldn't show, Erimon," a man's voice spoke from a shadowed corner of the room.

Erimon tensed at my side, those glacial eyes scanning the area. "Me? Not show? Sounds preposterous."

A deep, raspy chuckle followed, and the mysterious man

slunk from the darkness. He was everything I'd imagined a Druid to be. Light grey robes hung from his shoulders, dragging on the floor and covering his bare feet, his toes only poking out long enough for him to take labored steps forward. The sleeves were wide and billowing, his hair stark white with streaks of dark grey, draped to his hips, his long beard mixed in with it at the same length. He leaned on a gnarled cane positioned under one armpit and paused in front of us, his chocolate eyes sparkling as he took us in.

"Abigail, my dear." He reached a wrinkled, pale hand toward me, littered with a dozen liver spots. "I've been waiting a long time for you to be born."

A breath caught in my throat, and I looked to Erimon silently asking him if I should shake his hand, kiss his knuckles, or even curtsy, perhaps?

You can shake his hand, love.

Slipping my hand into the older man's, I offered a hearty smile. "The Elder, I presume?"

"Yes." After shaking, he curled both hands over the top of his cane and narrowed his eyes at Erimon. "And if it weren't for this little shit taking his sweet time getting his head out of his ass, you would've been brought into this world far sooner."

"I—" I'd forgotten how to speak after those words. My lips parted, begging to ask a question that I didn't know how to ask. "—wait—who were my parents?"

The Elder kept his gaze on Erimon, surveying him from head to toe as he talked to me. "That I do not know, I'm afraid. I only know they died when you were still a newborn. Faeries and starlight brought to foster care's doorstep to be raised as a human until you came into your true purpose."

I pressed a hand to my chest, my heart slamming against my ribcage. The tattoo sizzled my skin, crimson bursts of light fracturing from its lines. "But then, the Dullahan. Why would he mark me if he knows what I am?"

The Elder finally turned back to me, stroking a hand down the length of his beard and nodding. "He doesn't know. Not yet. The Dullahan was attracted to your essence because, for reasons he couldn't fathom, sensed you were a threat. And he'd be right."

Erimon moved closer to the Elder. "You've been planning this from the beginning, haven't you?"

The Elder's eyes brightened, and then amusement danced in his gaze. "And you've grown wiser too, it seems."

Covering my mouth with a hand to hide my smile, I stayed quiet, letting the two ancient Druids have their reunion without interference from me.

You're never an interference.

I elbowed Erimon in the side hard enough to make him grunt.

"Yeah, yeah. Out with it, Elder. I deserve to know what all of this—" He referenced our tattoos "—is about. Because you called it a *curse.*"

The Elder nodded, grunted, and sat on a log bench near the stony hearth ablaze at the back wall. "You wouldn't have walked this path if I hadn't told you otherwise, Erimon. We both know that."

Erimon raked a hand through his hair, tugging on it. "What *path?*"

He was frustrated, hopeful, and angry all in one breath, and it threatened to overwhelm me.

The Elder beat the brunt of his stick against the wooden floorboards, garnering our undivided attention. "I needed you to become selfless, boy. To become righteous and loyal. And above all else—" A blue light flashed in the Elder's eyes. "—I needed you to become a *leader* instead of the lone wolf you've insisted on being all these years."

Erimon twirled the rings on his fingers, his irritation and impatience growing, making *me* antsy. "You've still failed to explain *why*."

"You know the reason you just refuse to acknowledge it." The Elder beat his stick once more before using it to pull himself to standing. "It is time you take your place as High King, Erimon. Those worthy before you are dead, and no other comes after you. It *has* to be you."

The color drained from Erimon's face, and for the first time I could recall, he looked shell-shocked. He staggered back on his heels, and I reached an arm out to steady him, rubbing one of his shoulders. "I'd somehow always known in my gut, but it never made sense. How do I have the blood of the High Kings? My father, he wasn't—"

"Your great, great-grandfather was. Your father had always been the envious type. It's probably where you inherited that glowing part of your personality. The High King blood chooses who it passes down to, and your father wasn't chosen." The Elder tapped a finger against his cane, nodding as if thinking of some age-old memory.

"Does that mean he'll have to give up the life of a Druid?" I asked the question for him, knowing it was at the forefront of his mind.

Erimon's gaze focused on the Elder with the vulnerable hope of a boy at Christmastime.

"Of course, he can. We *need* him to be that Druid. Becoming High King doesn't change that. It never has. But he's never understood it because he's always failed to *listen*." The Elder pointed a stern, bony finger at my Druid.

Erimon curled his arm around my waist and rubbed a thumb between his eyes. "And what of Abby? You bring her into my life only to thrust me into the job and duties of High King?"

The Elder's lips curve into a gentle smile. "She's a part of you, isn't she? In fact, she's as just as much a part of all of this as you are. Tell me, when your wings first appeared, what had happened before it?" The Elder arched a bushy grey brow.

Gasping, I draped a hand over my mouth and gulped. "Our night in the bog, Erimon."

We'd made love for the first time in the garden, and the very next day, his wings had appeared, wings he never knew he possessed.

"Yes. You're a Druid High King. Those wings should've been your first clue. And you'd always gotten so frustrated over never being able to find your mate. That's because she needed to find *you* when the moment was right." The Elder rolled his right shoulder, grimacing, and coughing.

Erimon and I exchanged glances. The look of admiration, longing, and pride on his face had the ring resonating with a vibrant melody meant for only me to hear.

"She's to be your Druid Queen," the Elder finished.

Much like Erimon's moments prior, my knees went wobbly,

and Erimon steadied me. "When is this all supposed to be happening?" The words barely made it out from how coarse my throat had become.

The Elder scooped a leather-bound book into the crook of his arm, hobbling past us to the door. "I perform the ritual you've both come here for. I bond you. Then, with everyone else, you stop the Dullahan, break the chaos of this cycle, and return to the Hill for your coronations."

"Erimon." His name was a plea pushed from a shuddery breath as I collapsed against his chest.

Erimon held me tightly against him, his fingers combing my hair, the other hand kneading my back. "I know this is a lot, *luachmhar*. But once all of this is said and done, it'll be you and me. And there's no one I'd rather be going through this insanity with than *you*."

Tears pricked my eyes, and I peeled back, bunching his shirt in my hands. I let my eyes roam his head, imagining what a crown would look like there. How might the new position change the way he carried himself and the way he acted around others? And I dismissed it all because what kept me grounded was knowing it wouldn't change a *thing*. He'd still be the charismatic Druid I met at the pub—the one who managed to steal my heart and give me some of his in return.

"I'm certainly never one to rush, but we haven't much time," the Elder said after uncomfortably clearing his throat.

Erimon stepped back and held his hand out, palm up, for me to take. He pressed his lips to my knuckles, and the Elder led us to the only backdrop fit for a Druid bonding ceremony—the forest.

The sun had begun to set, painting the sky a light orange with dark purple and crimson streaks. Another night drew near and became another lasting reminder that the full moon grew closer. I'd have to face the Dullahan again. Only this time when this was over, I'd smile at his unmoving corpse.

The Elder led us into a circular, mossy patch devoid of trees, the branches full of vibrant emerald leaves, but not so much that fractals of light were able to trickle through. I interlaced my fingers with Erimon's, not wishing to let go of him for anything.

"If you both will stand within the center of the circle," the Elder beseeched, holding out his hand.

We turned toward each other, hands in hands, smiling, with our hearts beating the same erratic but excited rhythm.

"Miss Weber, please remove your ring so Erimon can use it as a token for the bonding." The Elder said, gesturing to the Claddagh ring adorning my right hand.

Nodding, I slipped it off and held it out for Erimon. He took it with a grin, and both our minds delved into that evening in the hole where he'd tricked me into letting him help me. The time when he'd already tied our destinies together before he knew for certain they were meant to be tied.

"Erimon, care to make a ring for yourself, or would you prefer another magical tattoo?" The Elder pointed at our Celtic sleeves, no amusement in his tone.

Erimon gazed at his left hand, where a gold ring with a square emerald gem rested on his ring finger. "I'll make a new ring." Grunting, he yanked away the one already occupying the coveted spot. "I was getting tired of this one anyway." With a sensual smile, he lifted the ring, its gold metal turning to dust in the wind, and he caught the emerald, slipping it in his pocket. He wriggled his fingers, pulling iron ore from the earth and spiraling it together in his palm until a simple iron band of Celtic knots appeared, and he held it out to me.

"It's beautiful, yet masculine." I curled my hand into a fist, securing it there as if it would float away. "Very fitting for you."

"And this attire, Bandruí—" Erimon brushed my hair away from my neck. "—simply won't do."

Erimon pressed his fingertips to my clothes, transforming them into the shimmering blue dress he'd made for me in the Bog. I stood barefoot with nothing on my skin save for the dress, and when my hair rustled once I turned my head, I felt for the source, pulling one between two fingers.

Green and golden leaves braided into my hair.

My grip loosened, and the wind took the leaf away, high into the air above us. "I'd seen myself like this in a vision, how could you have—"

"Because I saw it too." Erimon curled my hands under his chin. "Right as you did."

Smiling, resplendent, and over-joyed, I pressed my hand to Erimon's chest, willing my flames to turn his shirt and boots into embers. He was shirtless now, in only his pants, our toes both free to dig into the dirt beneath our heels.

Erimon's eyes formed his infamous squint. "Always desiring my shirt off, Abby. Naughty, naughty."

"It's how *I* now picture you as a Druid." Inching closer to him, it had become easy to forget the Elder stood a mere few paces away. We leaned in for a kiss.

The Elder coughed, jarring us. "Perhaps save it for the final step of the ceremony?"

What did I tell you? So many bleedin' rules.

I bit back a smile, but let my eyes twinkle in the sunset rays so he'd know I appreciated his candor and always will.

"You have to get back to the others as soon as possible, so I'm going to make this quick." The Elder slipped one hand over my shoulder, the faint thrumming of his magic already humming against my skin. "Do you, Abigail Weber, bind yourself to this Druid and future High King, in both mind and body, for all eternity, even if death falls upon either of you?"

"Yes," I said no sooner had the last word fallen from the Elder's lips. My tattoo sparked to life, a fiery trail starting from my wrist, working its way along the lines, and gradually making its way up my arm.

"And do you, Erimon, son of Mis Espione and rightful heir, bind yourself to this Bandruí, in both mind and body, for all eternity, to accept her as your High Queen, even if death falls upon either of you?"

Erimon's grip tightened on my hands. "Yes."

A blue beam of light, starting from Erimon's tattoo, spread through his arm, into the Elder, and surged into *me*. I gasped, wincing as the sensation bordered on pain, but it never fully got there.

"The rings now," the Elder encouraged, still holding onto us.

We took turns slipping the rings on each other's left hands, the tingling sensations growing tenfold, sizzling through my stomach and head. The light settled within my tattoo, and once the static feeling, radiating through every inch of my skin subsided, our tattoos glowed an equal mix of red and blue.

"By the power bestowed upon me as an ancient leader to the order of the Druids, I can vow this Druidic bond to be sound." The Elder released us and staggered back, gripping his cane to keep from falling entirely.

Erimon launched his arm to steady the much older Druid, concern for him cinching his brows.

The Elder batted his hand away. "I'm fine, I'm fine. You know how much energy a bonding ceremony consumes. Now kiss her, seal the bond, and *go* stop the Dullahan."

Erimon turned toward me, and my new body sang the loudest hymns to the very tops of the rolling Irish hills. I now knew what Phoebe meant when she'd said she felt whole after bonding with Patrick. All tiles fell into place, every corner my life had turned, and every waking moment since booking the trip to Ireland all settled into perfect understanding. I was free. And Erimon was *mine*.

Erimon wrapped his arms around me, planting such a fierce kiss on my mouth that it felt like a volcanic eruption consuming the earth with raging bursts of lava. I curled my hands to the back of his neck and leaned into him, not wishing to stop the kiss for anything.

Hesitantly, Erimon pulled away and traced his hardened fingertips down the exposed part of my back. "Let's stop the Dullahan first, my future queen. We have forever to be this, to be *us*."

Nodding while stifling a whimper, I reluctantly agreed.

Erimon scooped me into his arms, prepared to carry me over the ethereal threshold, but first turned to the Elder. "You've always been a crotchety old fart in my eyes, Elder, but I'd be lying if I said I wasn't thankful. For everything."

"Yes, yes. Just uphold your duty when you return, Druid." The Elder had sunk into the nearest chair, propping his arms on the cane.

Erimon smirked and muttered, "Crotchety old fart."

As if he knew I wanted nothing more than to see them, Erimon flared his falcon wings and nuzzled his nose to the side of my head. I stroked my fingers over the coarse feathers that led to the smaller, softer ones. And with his wings proudly displayed, Erimon ported us back to the stone where Morrigan, for the first time, couldn't help but express awe and admiration at the sight of us—the Druid duo.

13

ERIMON

THE HIGH KING.

It's in my *veins*.

I've surpassed my *father*.

And Abby was to be my High Druid *Queen*.

The words still circled in my brain, having never genuinely settled since the Elder revealed it all to me. If it weren't for being officially bonded to Abby, the thoughts alone may have distracted me more than I'd ever care to let on. But through the absurdity of it all, it didn't feel foreign, it felt like home, just a new dwelling that I would need to grow accustomed to with very little time to do it.

"You two are glowing," Morrigan said, snapping me from my whirlpool of thoughts. "*Literally* glowing."

Our tattoos still shone with a sparkling mix of red and blue, the parts that overlapped flashing purple for a nanosecond before continuing their trailing light dance. The way the tattoos glimmered seemed to suggest they felt whole again

110

after being separated for the greater good. The weight of the new bonding ring felt heavy on my finger, not because it was a burden, but because it wanted to remind me it was there. That what just transpired in the Hills of Tara with the Elder, who had been like a second father to me growing up, truly *happened.* And if I needed any further reassurance, my Abby, smiling at me, curled against my side, beaming from her inherited immortality, was more than any male could ask for.

"I'd say if it were too distracting, we'd turn it off, but I have no bleedin' idea how to do that." Glancing down, I realized I was still shirtless, and Morrigan hadn't batted an eyelash over it. "Maybe we should start with some clothes to cover them for now?"

Abby ran her hands over the twinkling blue dress I'd made for her months ago and never had the heart to toss away. "I stashed some extra clothes in Patrick's house. Just in case."

This Bandruí. This *woman* had already shared my soul and stolen my very being, but now she sought to claim my very existence.

Pressing a hand to my chest, I widened my eyes at Abby. "Me. Too."

"Yeah, alright. I'll meet you two back at the house, paramours." Morrigan snickered and swirled inky tendrils around her body to disappear in a flash of smoke and crow feathers.

Dragging the back of my hand over Abby's tattoo, I stifled a shiver that consumed me from the contact. "Before we go. How do you feel?"

"Is this a trick question?" She made a circle with her finger between my pecs.

Chuckling, I secured some of the dark hair hanging over her eyes behind her ear. "No. I've always been immortal. I'm only curious to know how it feels to go from thinking you don't have forever to suddenly having an eternity in front of you."

Abby opened her mouth to respond but then closed it, her face scrunching as if such a thought hadn't crossed her mind. "Is it absurd to say that I never thought about dying? That I never went to sleep at night thinking I may not wake up the next morning?"

"It was like some deep-seated side of you knew this was to come."

Thoughtfully, she nodded and started to chew on her thumbnail.

"As I told the Elder, it was the same for me and being High King. But I figured my father had talked so much about it in my youth. It was why I couldn't get it out of my mind."

Abby pressed a palm to my cheek, a grounding gesture I hoped she'd never stop giving me. "I'm here now, Erimon. We found each other, and now, we're going to end this—together."

After giving a stern nod, I ported us inside Patrick's hovel—a feat I'd never been able to do before, and not only did it catch me off guard, but everyone inside the house as well. They stared at me as if I'd just caught them in the middle of a secret orgy. The only being who made a sound was the raven, squawking in delight at the sight of Abby and flying to her outstretched hand.

"Great. Now you can barge your way into places, hm?" Patrick said, a bit of jest in his tone, a snarky, dimpled grin soon following.

Phoebe shrieked from the other side of the room and sprinted until she all but attacked Abby with a big bear hug. Abby stumbled backward, laughing and catching her best friend in a warm embrace.

Finn slammed his fist to the table and stood. "Look at Monny all grown up."

"More than you realize," I grumbled.

Mave moved closer, her eyes searching between me and Abby, her gaze focused on our matching glowing ink. "This is something uniquely special, isn't it?"

Nodding, I slipped a hand over her shoulder and patted her there before standing in the center of the room, ready to address the friends and acquaintances that would help bring Balor and the Dullahan to their knees. "Everyone, before we embark on this mission, I have an additional announcement."

Abby rubbed Phoebe's arms before slowly pulling away from the vice-grip hug Phoebe still had locked on her, laughing. Abby stood at my side, her scent and warmth washing over my skin like steam from a hot spring.

"Before the Elder completed the bonding ceremony, he requested I agree to something once we've defeated the Dullahan. To answer—a calling." My jaw set of its own accord. I glanced between the group, most of which seemed to lean in, eager to hear my reveal. "To become High King."

"Holy fuck," Cu said, his mouth falling slack for the first time in his ethereal existence.

Rhiannon stopped petting her unicorn's head long enough to flash me a shocked expression.

Finn barked in a hoot of laughter and slapped his knee. "I'll be damned. I'm tellin' ye I always knew there was more to Erimon than arrogance and assery."

"You're so full of absolute shit, Finn," Morrigan retorted, snorting and tilting back in her chair.

Patrick and Phoebe stood silent and perplexed, not realizing how big of a deal such a title was among the Celtic celestials.

Mave's cheek ticked, no doubt disguising a twinge of jealousy, but soon, she thumped her fist against her chest. "I'm honored to be a friend, your Maj—"

"Mave," I held up a palm to halt her. "I'm not sworn in yet."

Her expression melted, and she adjusted her sword's sheath. "Ah. In that case, I can still jerk you around until you are then."

"And Abby," I reached for her hand. "Is to be High Queen."

Gasps and utter silence filled the space, creating a choking sensation in the air.

"The Elder assured us this wouldn't change us being Druids, Erimon most of all," Abby continued without missing a beat.

"Well," Finn started, striding across the room until his gigantic hand clapped me on the shoulder. "I guess we need to keep your royal arse alive then, hm?"

A newly formed twinge of protectiveness for my people and worry for their safety over my own coiled in my gut. "No. I don't want any special treatment. Same as it's always been."

"Oh, Erimon." Mave chuckled and, in rare form, kissed my cheek. "You don't get a say in that. Not anymore. We are duty bound to protect our High King—" She glanced at Abby with a dipped chin. "—and Queen whether you've been officially announced or not."

Cu folded his burly arms. "You want us to be smited?"

"Smited?" I snickered and referenced the room filled with gods, goddesses, and heroes. "By who?"

"Lugh," Finn said.

"The Dagda," Mave added.

Rhiannon moved away from her unicorn long enough to chime in with, "Dian Cecht."

"Just to name a few," Morrigan finalized, a deviousness still playing in her words.

Frustration riddled my skin, and I found the nearest wall on which to lean. A deep sigh pushed from my lungs. The weight of being an ethereal leader already weighed as heavy as boulders on my limbs. "The Elder claimed nothing would change, yet *everything* will change."

Abby slipped behind me, her breasts pressing to my bare skin between my shoulder blades. Her arms wrap around me, hands curling at my shoulders and holding me tight, her chin resting at my nape. "Sometimes change is good, grá."

Love.

The murmurs of conversation from our counterparts turned to white noise in my ears. I turned to face her, my thumb skirting her jawline. "You spoke Gaelic."

Abby blinked several times as if she hadn't noticed. "I don't know Gaelic."

"You do now, grá. You do now." I pressed an all-consuming kiss to her lips, breathing her in and letting our bond dull my senses, clearing my mind.

Finn gave a loud, exaggerated clearing of his throat. "Would you mind puttin' on a damn shirt on Monny so we can get to the docks?"

Pulling away, but sliding Abby's bottom lip through mine, I kept my eyes shut for a moment, drinking the sensations in. "Patrick, did you commission a ship like I asked?"

"Aye. The captain will be waiting for us at half past midnight," Patrick answered.

"Captain? Should we really be letting some mortal stranger in on our plans?" Morrigan asked, disdain surrounding her symbolically forked tongue.

Moving past Phoebe and Patrick, I opened the wooden chest at the foot of their bed, pulling out two satchels. Abby even hid hers in the same damn place. After tossing one to Abby, I pulled out a fresh shirt, boots, and jacket. "We don't need the captain. We have a Hound."

Patrick squinted at us, pointing perplexedly at the wooden chest, and he and Phoebe shared quick, bewildering glances.

"Cu? You know how to sail?" Morrigan stood, a delightful surprise now gracing her expression.

Mave sighed and turned her gaze toward the heavens. "We didn't drown the last time he was at the helm. He has that much going for him."

Cu adjusted his belt and uncomfortably cracked his neck to one side. "Might be the first decent thing you've said to me, Mave."

Mave had been in mid-sip from her tankard, lowering it with cheeks full of liquid and a frown. "And I already regret it."

"I can render him unconscious long enough for us to pull out of port," Rhiannon announced with a far too cheery voice at the mention of knocking a human out.

A knot formed in my neck, and Abby, rubbed it with my asking, kneading it with her knuckles.

"Better plan than Mor running him through with her blade and leavin' him to bleed out on the dock," Cu said, grunting.

Morrigan was using said blade to file her nails into more deathly points, and she let the dagger go limp in her grasp. "I never said I'd do that."

"You never said you wouldn't either," Cu countered.

Morrigan pursed her lips and shrugged, busying herself with her nails again.

In my youth, I wouldn't have cared if it were raining, snowing, or a bleedin' hurricane, I'd have knocked the mortal out for my own gain and left them to fend for themselves. But I was to be a ruler now, a leader, a *king*.

"Rhiannon, I appreciate your participation. See to it that wherever he lay unconscious, he's free from harm or the elements." For whatever reason, I'd dropped my voice an octave when giving this command.

Rhiannon bowed her head and then raised to the balls of her feet. "The boat is big enough for Estrella, correct?"

The unicorn huffed and scraped a hoof against the wooden floorboards. Patrick grimaced and dragged a hand down his face, eyeballing the scratch marks left behind by the action.

"I'm sure we'll manage." Reaching for Abby's hip, I led her in front of me.

We both know Phoebe can't join us on this quest. It's too dangerous for her and everyone else, with her having no powers or means to defend herself.

Abby nodded and patted my chest.

Let me take this burden for you.

And with those few words spoken by my mate, the changes

seemed superfluous and minor.

Abby crossed the room to Phoebe, and soon they were both frowning, but Phoebe's shoulders drooped, and it seemed she understood. I'd never given Phoebe enough credit. Not only did she do us all a huge favor by marrying a leprechaun she'd only known for days, but she'd remained upbeat and carefree, maintaining her jubilant personality through it all.

Once Abby returned to me, I snaked an arm around her waist. "Everyone ready?"

Mumbles and grunts floated throughout the room, Finn's grumbling the loudest of them all. But soon, everyone was touching shoulders, arms, or hands, ready for me to port our jolly group to the docks.

Except, of course, Morrigan.

"Yes, yes, Mor. We'll meet you there," I said before she had the chance.

Morrigan grinned and patted my cheek, the second pat more like a light slap. "You catch on so quickly, Druid. You'll do just fine in your new role."

As I ported us to the docks, the brightened moon hanging full and resplendent in the starlit velvet sky, we stared at the ship resting at the docks, its sails drawn up, ready to unwind and carry us to the Ninth Wave.

Taking a moment to stare at the mighty vessel, I thought back to our first means of transportation, the lime green clown car Patrick had procured, and realized just how far we'd come. Now, *this* majestic wooden steed floating silently in the murky waters would take us to the Dullahan to end his crusade once and for all.

14

ERIMON

"TELL ME AGAIN WHY THE unicorn is on board and taking up half of the bleedin' shoulder room?" Finn asked, grunting as he adjusted himself in the corner of the deck.

"Where I go, Estrella goes. We feed each other power. I wouldn't be near as useful to you all without her." Rhiannon hugged the unicorn's neck before kissing it.

"Yes, because you've done *so* much for us thus far," Morrigan spat, disdain evident in her tone.

Abby sat between my legs, resting her back against my chest while I propped against the mast. "Mor," I warned, tossing her an arched brow and a deliberately slow finger wag.

Morrigan held her palms in surrender and turned away with a flick of her black and crimson robes. "I'm going to coil some rope or something.

Cu had his back to us, gripping the ship's edge and making continued sounds like he was about to vomit but never did more than a dry heave. Abby's raven had been hopping on the

119

railing, cawing at the occasional fish that'd leap to the surface, and squawking and flapping its wings in protest when it didn't have time to catch it.

"Emrys is probably starving." Abby patted my knee before standing and moving toward the ship's edge with the raven. She extended her hand toward the seas, and within mere moments, several fish appeared on deck, flopping.

How quickly Abby was coming along with her powers. She'd taken what most Druids need a decade to master and crammed it into a matter of months. And given everything that'd been revealed as of late, I couldn't help but wonder if this, too, was by design.

The ocean waves beat against the hull, wind kicking up the sails and catapulting us closer to the Ninth Wave breakpoint. I beat the back of my head against the mast, attempting to distract myself from this growing impatience gnawing at my bones.

"How much longer do you figure, Mor? And if you don't say a matter of hours, I may lose my fantastical mind." I pinched the bridge of my nose, awaiting the answer I wholeheartedly didn't wish to hear.

Morrigan licked her finger and held it up. "It should be a matter of hours. There are some fierce winds over the Irish Sea today. Those nature sprites must be helping their future High King get to his destination faster, hm?"

All but rolling my eyes, I beat my head against the mast once more for good measure. "They're not *sprites*."

"What are they, then?" Rhiannon asked, her expression resembling a curious child's.

I sat up straight and hitched a knee to my chest. "I don't

know how to describe it. An essence?"

"So, you haven't actually seen how nature manifests itself?" Mave chimed in, joining the other two females with her arms crossed.

Pushing to my feet, I flipped the lapels of my jacket around my face. "How could I see it? It's wind, it's air, it's a fleck of dirt or sand."

"If you haven't seen it, how are you so sure it's *not* composed of sprites?" Patrick, who had been scarce prior to this coup, said from nowhere.

"Because—" Abby started, joining me at my side. "Sprites and faeries are sequestered to the Bog. Considering nature is everywhere in the known universe, I'd feel *very* confident saying our powers do not manifest through sprites."

Morrigan's face flattened, Patrick snickered, and Finn looked like someone just took a steamy shit in his blood pudding.

"Bleedin' bond. Ruining all the fun," Mave mumbled, turning to busy herself with rigging.

There was no stopping the resplendent grin spreading across my lips. "And now she saves *me*."

"You get that one." Abby trailed her touch up my arms, starting at my wrists, and didn't stop until she reached my neck, curling her hands around it. "The rest will cost ye."

Sucking air through my nose, I tried desperately to focus on rational thought, but her scent filling the space between us had my finger dipping into the back of her pants right above her ass. "Mm, and what will serve as payments?"

"I'm sure you will think of something—" Abby tilted her chin, her breath moistening my ear before she nibbled the lobe. "—satisfactory."

"Look lively," Morrigan barked, pointing to the massive tidal wave forming in the distance. "Did I say hours? I meant—*now*."

The raven flew to Abby's shoulder, and we moved to the front of the ship, gazing in awe over witnessing the Ninth Wave for the second time for most of us and the first for others, Abby included. She moved as close as she could get, leaning over the ship's side, the water ascending to the skies, misting her cheeks.

With the unicorn trailing on her heels, Rhiannon joined Abby at the bow. "Chlíodhna," she yelled.

The rest of us went stone-cold silent, glancing at each other, clueless about what to do other than watch Rhiannon do what she said she'd do. And Rhiannon, with the forbearance of a saint, waited several heartbeats before calling for the Banshee Queen a second time. When the only answer remained a wave so high you couldn't see the end of it edging closer and closer, the unicorn shook its mane, making sparkles and stardust plume from it.

A figure began to emerge from the wave's center—a female with radiant blonde hair falling in loose waves to her knees. A flowered crown circled her head, and a flowing sky-blue dress with golden embroidery clung to her floating form. I'd never met Chlíodhna in the flesh, but there was no mistaking this was her.

"Rhiannon," Chlíodhna said, but her lips didn't move, nor did her throat bob. She spoke through the sea breeze, and it carried her words to us.

Rhiannon curtsied, the unicorn following by bending one

knee and lowering its head. "My Queen. We've come seeking safe passage through the Wave."

Chlíodhna's glowing, pale blue eyes scanned our group, her expression remaining neutral and calm. "To what purpose?"

"Abigail, the Bandruí next to me, destined to become High Queen and bonded to Erimon, destined High King, has been marked by the Dullahan. She can put an end to his current cycle." Rhiannon kept her chin dipped, gaze fixed on the floorboards.

Chlíodhna's focus turned to Abby, the water bordering her body bubbling and frothing. Abby stood frozen as if entranced by the banshee, and though my limbs ached to ensure her safety, I stayed where I was, trusting her new power.

"And what do you offer for my cooperation?" Chlíodhna asked, turning her attention back to Rhiannon.

Rhiannon extended her palms, several golden apples appearing in her hands in a shimmer of white leaves and swirling silver dust. "Golden apples. For your birds. I know how they're hard to come by now."

A hint of a smile edged at Chlíodhna's lips before fading just as quickly. "I accept this as a tribute. You are free to pass through the Wave, but know this—in the Otherworld, you are to do nothing but defeat the Dullahan if you can lure him there. Talking to anyone else, taking anything, or altering the Otherworld in any way will result in you remaining *there*."

Patrick gulped and pulled at his shirt's neckline. The greedy Leprechaun probably hoped there'd be no shiny coins to tempt him over there.

"You have our word," Rhiannon answered for the lot of us.

The apples disappeared in water droplets, floating until they reached Chlíodhna.

"Be quick. Be just," were the last words Chlíodhna spoke before the wave consumed her.

"Well, that certainly beat fightin' off the damned Femori again." Finn chuckled, his laughter dying when no one joined him.

"Hardly seems fair the *Banshee* Queen gets to look so godsdamned gorgeous," Morrigan scoffed, kicking an empty bucket across the deck.

Finn rubbed the back of his neck as he drew closer to Rhiannon and the unicorn. "Oh, I don't know. I've seen far more beautiful creatures."

Mave rested her hands on her sword's pommel. "Maybe if you used less charcoal around your eyes, Mor, you'd look less like death incarnate?"

Morrigan's daggers appeared in her hands in a flash, and she twirled them into an attack position, storming across the boat toward Mave.

"You really want to do this now, Countess of Crows?" Mave drew her sword.

"Enough," I roared, my voice reverberating off the wood, the sails, the sea itself.

All went quiet, weapons were sheathed, and attention from the entire group turned to me.

"Passing the Ninth Wave was the first of our problems. We need to convince the Dullahan and Balor to follow us through it. The Dullahan must be in the Otherworld for this to work."

"I stay," Abby said, all heads whipping to the front of the ship, where she still stood gaping at the awaiting Wave.

"What?" I whispered, unable to control the way my head shook in protest.

Abby turned, her eyes locking with mine, the raven rubbing its head on her cheek.

Listen to me, Erimon. Truly listen.

"The odds of the Dullahan appearing on a ship in the middle of the Irish Sea only to battle a band of gods and heroes is slim." As Abby walked toward me, the gang parted for her like a seam unraveling. "Me alone? Claiming I attempted this by myself because I feared for my friends' safety? For my mate's safety? There is no other way."

"But Abby, that's madness. What if the Dullahan strikes, and your powers don't react as fast as they should? I believe in ye, I do, but—" Finn said, a deep frown wrinkling his features.

"The Dullahan won't have a chance to strike because I'll call for Erimon, and he'll be there as soon as I ask," Abby said with such sheer certainty, that it was enough to make my chest tighten.

"And how do you plan to do that if we're already through the Wave?" Morrigan asked.

"They can talk through each other's heads or some shite," Finn answered, the rest of the group gasping, arching brows, and shooting bewildered expressions my way.

"Did you ever plan to tell us that?" Mave threw her hands to her hips.

Closing the remaining distance between me and Abby, I hugged her to me, sputtering from some of the raven's feathers getting in my mouth. "It wasn't important at the time, Mave, but yes, I'll be able to hear Abby even from the Otherworld. The bond strengthened our mystical tether."

"What are we waiting for?" Morrigan gestured toward the Wave.

Usually, I'd find her lack of empathy chaotic and misplaced in situations such as these, but given our narrow timeframe, I had to agree with her this one time.

"Alright, grá. As soon as you're able to pull them over, reach out to me. As *soon* as you're sure. You hear me?" I rested my forehead against hers, fighting the urge to say anything more. She was my equal, my mate, and my soon-to-be Queen. Her passion and confidence were traits that pulled me toward her even in the beginning, and I couldn't expect her to change that—I didn't *want* her to change.

"You have my word, Druid. I quite value my life," Abby whispered, pressing a quick peck to my lips and rubbing the jacket sleeve that covered her tattoo against my own.

The matching inks hissed against our skins, begging for closer contact. Before I couldn't stand it any longer, I let go of her and stepped back, giving a solemn nod.

"Everyone, let's go. That's an order," I commanded.

As soon as you can.

Abby stood firm, the raven perched proudly on her shoulder, refusing to abandon her. She kept her back to us as we stood on the ship's railing, and I, with my Druidic gifts bestowed on me ages ago, ported us through the Ninth Wave without hesitation. Because Abby would contact me when the time was right—a phantom whisper only *I* could hear.

15

ABBY

I'D KEPT A STERN BUT neutral face when the group ported through the Ninth Wave, but my shoulders slumped, my knees buckling no sooner were they out of sight. I couldn't have fathomed meeting Erimon's gaze, so I didn't know if he had tried. But my gut instinct told me he couldn't risk doing it either. An eternal bond was unlike anything I'd ever experienced. Its ties were more potent than any shared blood or time with another person. It was an invisible tether that remained taut despite any distance between you. And that aching, quivering tightness pained my head, stomach, and heart when he drifted to the Otherworld, and I remained on Earth.

The ship lulled with the rolling waves beneath its hull, the Wave before it towering like a glittering water giant with its arms stretched above its head. But it didn't threaten to devour us or crash us into the nearby jagged rocks, thanks to Rhiannon bartering us with safe passage, a bargain with the Banshee Queen. I knelt on the deck with Emrys screeching on my shoulder, staring at the mystical wonder, and waited. Waited for the irresistible lure of my chosen essence to fool them—the one to break the cycle. Aside from my connection with Erimon, knowing he'd always have my back no matter if we were lightyears apart, what kept me going was the knowledge that Dullahan had no idea he chased his *demise.*

It wasn't raining, but the constant mist from the Wave was enough to coat the ship's wood in a thin layer of moisture. My hair and clothes felt damp, and Emrys ruffled his feathers, ridding them of collected water beads. Sighing, I shifted to my ass and propped my forearms on my knees, humming a Gaelic song that I hadn't recalled knowing before today.

Thugamar féin a Samhradh linn.

Erimon's voice was like a trickle of liquid after walking in the unrelenting desert heat. It was blissful and needed but only left me ravenous for more.

Did you all make it?

I'm fine. How are you?

It unsettled me how Erimon skirted around my exact question, redirecting to declare that he was fine. But I couldn't let myself read too far into it. My mind had to be clear and alert when the Death gods arrived.

I could be better. But such are the ways of fabled heroes, hm?

It hadn't come through as strong as thought-out words, but the slightest hint of a whispered chuckle caressed down my neck.

Not even immortal for a day and already considering yourself a fable?

Emrys hopped from my shoulder to walk the perimeter of the ship, pecking at possible food remnants left behind.

I grew up on stories like us. Only then I didn't think any of it was real. I feel with every beat of my ethereal heart, we're meant to exist but remain in the shadows as a fantasy for the rest of the world to escape.

Propping on my elbows, I tilted my chin at the Wave, letting more of its glittering water coat my skin.

I'll say it again, you, Abigail Weber, are a treasure.

As hard as I tried not to think about it, his flippancy left a pit in my stomach.

Erimon, are the others alright?

He didn't answer straight away, and my skin prickled with nerves. I sat up, welcoming Emrys onto my lap, when he noticed my distress.

They made it through, Abby. You need to concentrate on Balor and Dully. They should be there any moment.

I chewed on my thumbnail until Emrys's head bobbing at my palm made me stop. He kept nudging my hand until I used it to stroke his feathers. The softness and sleekness instantly calmed my bubbling anxiety. Just as my bones settled, relaxing with the steady sounds of the water lapping against the boat—a familiar chill shot down my spine. I opened my eyes and spun to standing, only to be met with the sight of Dullahan in his Crom form. And no doubt the being standing next to him was Balor.

They're here. Listen for me, grá.

Always.

"Well, well," Balor started, shifting his long white hair over one shoulder and pacing from one side of the deck to the other. "At last, we meet Abigail. I must say—" He leaned back, his gaze scanning me from my feet to my face. "You certainly don't look like much."

"If we all judged power by appearance, I wouldn't give you any more clout than a newt." My tattoo hummed beneath my jacket, its red glow so radiant that some of it spilled from where my sleeve met my wrist. I pinched it shut. I couldn't reveal the very real ace up my sleeve just yet.

Balor let out a hooting laughter and slapped his thigh. "Ah, ha. Such fire. I see now why you were so drawn to her, Crom."

Crom's beady black gaze focused on my arm, the skin beneath one eye twitching. "It wasn't only that, Balor. There's always been something else about her I couldn't quite put my finger on."

In a blink, Balor appeared in front of me. I raised my fists, poised to fend them off as long as necessary to wait for them both to touch me. "You really think you could win this without a fight?"

"Foolish girl. You have an entire crew of beings willing to give up their immortal lives to save you, gods only know why, and yet you have the idiocy to be alone on the night of a full moon—a blood moon." Balor lifted a pale finger and swayed it, making a chastising *tsking* sound.

Not lowering my hands, I took a calculated step backward. "That's precisely why I'm alone. You both want *me*. No reason the rest of them should suffer for it."

Crom shoved past Balor, his nostrils flaring, taking a deep inhale of the scent spiraling around me. "The Druid. You're— *mated*."

"What?" Balor roared, pulling Crom behind him and

edging closer to me, sniffing for himself. "When in the fuck did you have time to do all that?"

I had them angry. Good. All the more reason for them to attack me, for me to put my powers to the test before the actual fight happened after luring them to the Otherworld.

"Mortals tend to work quickly when our lives are in the balance. As do—" I called on just enough of my power to make my eyes spark red. "—their mates."

It was Crom's turn to roar, but his shook me to my bone marrow. Balor could claim any ruling over the dead he chose, but the Dullahan would always be death incarnate, and his cries of agony turned the wails of wandering spirits into a macabre hymn.

"She's immortal," Crom said through clenched teeth, his slender, gnarled hands shaking at his sides.

Balor arched a bleached brow at me. "How?"

Be ready, Erimon.

Just say the word, Bandruí, and I'm there before you can finish the thought.

Glancing between them with a defiant, smug expression, I remained silent.

Balor sucked in a breath before launching at me and grabbing my shoulder, shaking me. I grinned, and his anger erupted into fury, the varying wrinkles in his forehead and cheeks deepening as his lip pulled back, snarling.

One out of two.

Standing tall with my chin poised, I let my power go into a frenzy. "The Elder Druid saw all of it. He knew from my birth as a mortal that I was to be *re*-born a Bandruí. The warrior

Druid's fated mate and his future—" The fiery magic burned through my jacket, leaving only the opposite sleeve intact. The tattoo pulsed red with hints of blue, but with Erimon so far away, they faded. "—High Queen."

Crom charged forward, so close to touching me but keeping enough distance that I couldn't reach him. "No. You hiss lies, witch. My mark wouldn't appear on an immortal, let alone a Bandruí."

Fear. A smidgen of desperation. Absolute fury. It all catapulted through Crom's expression as his limbs shook uncontrollably.

Lifting my wrist so he could see his death mark, the only spot of ink not glowing red because it wasn't from Erimon, I smirked at Death. "It's still there. You are still bound to capture and kill me, and we will fight you until time is no more, trumpets sound, or for the rest of eternity if need be."

Crom's chest heaved, and his hands flew toward my throat. *Now.*

Crom's nibbly fingers wrapped around my neck, and they never had the chance to tighten. Erimon appeared in a beam of blue light, swirls of autumn leaves wafting around him. He wrapped his arms around me from behind, and in the next instance, the ship, the sea, and the Ninth Wave all disappeared.

I'd landed on my hands and knees, my fingers digging into wet black sand. Emrys had flown to my shoulder at the precise moment, as if our minds were connected, and was still perched there, cawing at our surroundings. Scents of death, sulfur, and burning wood scattered the air, and feeling far too alone for comfort, a sudden panic surged down my spine.

Pushing to my feet, I did several circles, squinting at the unending darkness with only the occasional dimly lit sconce illuminating the space. Summoning my power, I willed a fireball to my palm, using it as a torch, and took tentative steps forward. The tattoo glowed crimson, but the resplendent cerulean patterns that once appeared were still faded. I'd just seen him. He took us through the Wave. Crom and Balor were both right *there*.

But Erimon wasn't there; worse—I couldn't *feel* him. The reality had me whimpering, choking on my own breath. The black sand shoreline seemed to go on forever, an oily midnight river lapping silently against it. Everything was so quiet, too quiet. There were no water droplets like in a cave, no echoes, no tiny squeaks from bats hanging from a rock ceiling.

I was thankful that Crom and Balor weren't caught in this hellscape with me, but they could be with Erimon or any of the others. Not one of us could take them on alone. We needed to do it as a united front. It couldn't end like this. An eternity alone? In nothingness? No. The Elder wouldn't have gone through all this trouble only for it to wither away into desolate blackness.

"Erimon?" I called out.

No response.

Erimon.

I thought of his name with such confidence. As if our phantom whisper could never fail. But that, too, received no answer. My anger and terror made the flame in my hand swell and spark. I gulped, controlling it. The last thing I needed was to set fire to whatever this place was and get caught in my own damned flames.

Emrys cawed, flapping his wings at something behind us. With eyes widened and alert, I spun on my heel, jutting out my hand to light up the opposite direction. Despite there being nothing, Emrys continued to have a fit on my shoulder—squawking, flapping, and pointing his beak skyward with chitters and chatters.

Squinting against the blanket of darkness, I took tentative steps forward and tried again. "Erimon?" It came out hesitant and low, unlike before when I'd shouted it to the heavens.

But the answer I received this time wasn't what I expected, nor wanted. The voice that responded was made up of a dozen voices—male, female, high-pitched, low-pitched, slower, frantic, maniacal. And they all repeated the same word over and over to the point it was skull-splitting.

Bandruí.

16

ERIMON

WE'D ALL MADE IT THROUGH the Ninth Wave without fail, but as soon as we appeared in the Otherworld, I realized I was alone. Yelling into the void or running laps within the darkness didn't do any good. Only I could hear myself, and moving felt like an endless loop. My other half, Abby, was also alone and *not* in the Otherworld. When I'd first called her through our bond, I'd done so with pinched eyes, praying this separation didn't affect that either. When she'd instantly responded, it was sweeter than a pixie's melody during the dawn of spring.

I hadn't let on that the others were missing. What else should I have done? She needed her head focused on how to handle Dully and Balor. My mate is fiercely loyal to those she cared about, and I knew if she thought for a moment any of us were in danger, she'd prioritize a rescue mission. But she didn't realize that I, the crew, maybe not Morrigan, but the rest of the gang, *even* Cu, had made *her* the priority.

When she'd spoken the word "now" into my mind, I pulled at nature's energy to surge it with my own and get me there that much faster. Had I stopped to think that the same thing would happen to me and Abby when crossing the threshold? Call me a lovestruck idiot, but here I thought our mating tether would somehow keep us together. It had not. The Otherworld gave no two shits about mates. That much was clear.

She'd been right there in my arms. I could smell her flowery perfume and the strawberry sweetness floating from her skin. And when I'd appeared back in the unending darkness, my hands were empty—devoid of that part of my soul she carried—again. The ink on my arm had given a delightful tingle when reunited with its counterpart. Now, it burned, ached, and sizzled, letting me know far too well what it thought of the situation.

Hissing, I rubbed my skin through the sleeve and clenched my teeth. Her scent still hung in the air for a few heartbeats before floating away entirely.

With a frustrated growl, I cried out, "Abby."

But it was the same as before. Nothing answered. Not even my voice bounced from what would be stone walls if this were a typical cave. Was it a cave? I had no fucking clue, but my irritation and impatience grew by the second.

Swallowing it down, I crouched to the sand, pressing a knee into the wet granules before pressing my fingertips to it and taking a deep, calming breath.

Abby.

Utter, irritating, silence.

Pissed beyond rational thought now, I stormed to my feet,

kicking a plume of sand with my boot. "For Elder's sake. We could talk to each other from different realms but not in the same one?"

I wasn't sure who I was talking to, but asking anything to nothing made me feel better than wallowing over it.

"And here I thought my day had gotten sour," an eerily familiar male voice spoke from the shadows.

Turning on my heel, I pulled sand in spirals to my palms, ready to use it as a slashing weapon if necessary. "Who are you?"

The male chuckled and moved into the dim lighting under one of three sconces, his hands folded behind his back. "Didn't recognize my voice?"

Fucking Balor.

"You say yours hasn't gotten sour, and I say mine has turned to shite in a handbasket." I formed a thin line of sand in front of me, holding it steady, ready to slice and dice Balor if he so much as flicked a finger in my direction.

"I wouldn't say all that. I'm glad we ran into each other here. Gives us a chance to talk." Balor smiled—a fucking pleasant grin as if we were old chaps preparing to sit down for tea and biscuits and discuss politics.

Shaking my head, I twirled my fingers, making the sand grains dance within the suspended line. "The only talkin' I wish to do with you, Balor, is with your corpse when I've figured out a way to end your immortal life for the second time."

A raspy chuckle punched from Balor's chest, and he stepped forward, making me tense. "I think you'll find it harder to bring me to my end when fate gave me a second chance. I quite prefer it on the surface."

"Perhaps you should've thought of that the first time around. And what a bang-up job you've done divin' into the old territory right out the gate. You know, the one that got you in trouble in the first place?" Testing him, I launched a sand spear toward Balor's left shoulder.

Balor leaned to the right and waved a finger at me. "Now, now, Druid. No need for things to get messy. I have to admit, I was quite impressed with your female. Not only did she trick us into the Wave, but she's accomplished so much in *such* a short time."

I didn't like his tone. Not one bit. It was condescending, aloof, and disinterested.

"Then you should know your time here is fleeting."

Dozens of whispers scattered through my mind suddenly, the intensity of it enough to make me wince and lose control of the sand. Gripping my head, I stumbled back on my heels.

"The mating bond isn't as strong when you two are apart. Correct me if I'm wrong, but you seem to be *missing* something or some*one*." Balor inched closer.

I flew my palm at him, attempting to launch a wave of sand that only managed to materialize into inconvenient wisps at his face. "Doesn't matter. We'll find each other, and when we do—"

"You've failed to remember." Balor had appeared at my side at some point between the pain surging through my skull and stating Abby's obvious non-presence.

A tight pressure pinched the skin at my wrists, the whispers in my head gradually dying off.

"Though this realm puts us on a more even playing field, and you have a far better chance at defeating us than in the mortal realm—" Balor leaned toward my ear. "—I can speak to the dead and give them a voice. And many of them are *very* lonely."

Grimacing, I yanked at the taut metal cursing my wrists—*the* golden shackles. "You think a pair of cuffs and some grim conversation will be enough to do me in?"

"I certainly hope not, or I've grossly underestimated you." Balor tugged on the cuffs' chain, leading me like a godsdamned dog into the darkness. "But this will ensure you don't try to skewer me with sand and keep you from speaking with your Bandruí."

Fuck it all to hell.

Abby, can you hear me?

Nothing. Silence.

Calling on my earthen metal powers, I attempted to melt the shackles, but Ilmarinen's enchantment prevented me or any other magical creature from tampering with them. This was happening. Balor was taking me hostage. I had no idea where my mate or the rest of my crew were, and Balor wanted to have a *chat*. I could only hope Abby would still somehow sense me, find me, and plunge a fireball straight into this prick's chest cavity.

"I used to have a small study—" Balor turned a corner and felt the stone wall until landing on one rock in particular. "—ah yes, here we are. It's been some time. I wasn't sure I'd remember which one it was." He laughed again, fucking chuckled, the dick.

"How fortunate," I mumbled. "I'd hate for us to have a civil conversation in a musty alcove."

The stone wall parted to one side, revealing a dimly lit room with wall-to-wall bookshelves filled to the brim with texts, a wooden table with four chairs in the center, and a metal candelabra with melted candles, one of them somehow still lit after all this time.

"See? We do agree on some things." Balor motioned for me to walk through first.

Gripping the chain tightly, hoping I'd find the strength to break it but couldn't, I acquiesced and crossed the threshold. What the hell else was I supposed to do?

Abby. Grá. Bandruí. Abigail.

I tried them all, sending them into the ether with the dwindling hope she'd hear one. And I kept repeating them until Balor slid the stone door shut, sealing us inside.

17

ABBY

BANDRUÍ. BANDRUÍ. BANDRUÍ.

Over and over again, the voices kept shrieking, wailing, crying out the word. I pressed the heels of my palms to my ears, trying to drown them out, but they only got louder. Collapsing to my knees, I pressed my hands against my skull until it ached.

"Please, stop. Shut up. Shut up." I'd started it as a subtle plea, but the ear-deafening pain became a dagger carving into my head, and I could barely stand it, so I screamed the last bit of it.

Emrys squawked and cawed at our surroundings in a helping effort but it only made the cacophony of noises more chaotic.

The voices didn't stop. They kept going, unrelenting and erratic. Did they want me to say something? Do something?

Gulping the pain away, I forced myself to stand, bubbling the fire in my palm. "Yes. I'm a Bandruí."

The repeated words turned into gasps and unintelligible

whispering. A few moments passed like this until it stopped abruptly, and blissful silence filled the darkness. I never thought the deathly quiet would be so welcoming.

"Why are you here?" A female voice, distant and wavering, said from behind me.

Still holding the awaiting fireball in my hand, I turned toward the sound. A ghostly mirage floated above the sand— purple hues and the faint outline of a woman's ghoulish face, a hood covering most of it. She had long, straggly hair that blended with the tattered robes that fell past her feet—if she had them because she was floating.

"I'm—" A shiver overtook me from a chill wrenching my spine. "—who are you?"

The figure moved closer, dozens of female whispers following until she was a breath away from me. "I am Vesta. The first of her kind."

The first Bandruí.

No longer feeling threatened, I doused the flame and bowed my head. "I only recently discovered I'm a Bandruí. I had to die and be reborn for it to manifest."

"My child, that's how all Bandruí come to be." Vesta stood motionless save for her billowing robes. "But again, why are you here? It is not your time."

I wished more than anything to see her expression. Would she be smiling if more than a skeleton remained?

"The Dullahan marked me when I was still mortal. I'm to put an end to his cycle. Me along with several heroes and—"

Vesta interrupted me by saying, "Erimon."

The mention of his name punctured my heart, and I pressed a

hand over my chest. Gods. Where *was* he? Where was everyone?

"Yes. How did you know?"

The question seemed more absurd when I asked it out loud, but I had *so* many questions.

"For over two thousand years, I have known you were to be born, Abigail. And yes, you were predefined by the stars to join forces with Erimon, the warrior Druid, to end this cycle's Dullahan chaos. But—" Vesta paused, her chin tilting downward. "—you were never meant to be marked by him."

I lifted my wrist, staring at the circle with the skull given to me by Death. Holding it out for her to see, I frowned. "Does this mean I can't defeat him?"

"You *can* and you *will* with the connection you share with the Druid." Vesta paused, her hood tilting to one side. "I sense there's more than a forged partnership?"

My lips had suddenly grown as dry as the Sahara and I licked them. Emrys settled on my shoulder, pointing his wings at the ghostly figure. "We're eternally bonded. We're—mates."

Considering everything else this being knew, I found it hard to believe she hadn't seen this one coming.

Síoraíocht.

The scattered whispers kept repeating this, some saying it calmly while others shrieked it.

Eternity.

"The Elder kept his word then, it would seem." Vesta joined the sleeves of her robes together as if interlacing her skeletal fingers within them.

I ran a finger over Emrys' crest, ignoring the tattoo's stinging radiating through my arm, reminding me that the very bond

I spoke of was still nowhere close enough to us. "His word?"

"You were the culmination of an agreement between me, the first Bandruí, and the Elder, one of the original Druids. I knew you were to possess great power, but my magic could only reach so far. The Elder was to ensure that Erimon would become your fated bond."

Síoraíocht. Síoraíocht.

The unsettling urge to ask the question looming over me since childhood that no one could answer still tugged at my curious heartstrings. Emrys rubbed his head against my cheek, encouraging me to ask her.

"My birth parents. Do you know who they were?"

"Yes." She'd said it so quickly it caught me off guard, making me rock back on my heels.

Hot tears stung my sinuses, and I took a harsh gulp to hold them back. "Can you tell me anything about them? Anything at all?"

Vesta floated around me as she spoke. "Your father was fae and your mother a Bandruí. You're the first of your kind, Abigail."

A fae father?

Despite my rounded ears, I felt for pointed ones I didn't inherit.

"Your unique fae blood is what gives you the potential to be the most powerful Bandruí in history."

The same words Morrigan had said to me.

"I don't understand. What about Morrigan or Rhiannon or countless other females with similar powers?"

The ghostly figure's hood shook left to right. "Goddesses. Not

Bandruí. Powerful in their own right, but not in the same way."

My head began to spin. I had learned so much about myself and my past in *such* a short amount of time.

"You must go and find your Druid mate, Abigail. Once you two are together, the rest of your party will follow." Vesta moved in front of me, the darkness lurking in her cloak's hood mesmerizing me.

"I don't know where he is. We can't communicate here like we do everywhere else. I can't—" Pinching my eyes shut, I ignored the hissing pain from the ink's disapproval against my skin. "—I can't *hear* him."

"Yes, you can. Listen more closely," Vesta whispered before her ghostly mirage disappeared, passing *through* me and making me gasp.

I'd half expected the ancient Bandruí to have branded me somehow like the Dullahan. But after inspecting my tattoo, it remained the same. Only now, she left me with more burning questions and an untapped power begging to be set free.

Crouching to my knees, I took a deep, meditating breath, focusing my concentration on my heartbeat and the sound of air going in and out of my nose.

I am a fae Bandruí.

I am the first of my kind.

I was carved from the stars and destined to find Erimon.

He was fated to become the male he was always meant to be with me at his side.

We are High King and Queen.

And if I can harness my power, I will be the most powerful Bandruí in the known cosmos.

I wouldn't know what else to do if these revelations weren't enough to heighten our celestial tether.

Pressing my fingertips to the sands, I calmed my thoughts, dipping into white noise and a blanketed mind, fully open for Erimon's whispered words.

For several pain staking moments, I heard nothing but Emrys' feathers ruffling and his beak ticking as he cleaned himself. Pushing those distractions away, I focused on my heartbeat, attempting to synch with Erimon's same steady rhythm. I stayed like this for the better part of an hour. My knees ached from staying in one spot on the sand, and a pain throbbed in my temple, but I *never* gave up.

And through all my efforts, pain, and focus, I finally heard him.

Grá. I'm trying again.

His voice was the loudest it had ever been in my mind, and I fell back on my ass, bouncing against the sand, my eyes flying open. Laughter pushed from my lungs, tears filling my eyes, and I kissed the top of Emrys's head.

"I know where he is, Emrys."

18

ERIMON

"WAIT, LET ME GUESS, THEN the bloke asked for directions despite being dead?" I asked, my palms flat on the table, leaning in my chair toward Balor with intrigue.

"Yes," Balor said, roaring with laughter.

I joined him, slapping my hand against the table and wiping a tear from my eye with a knuckle.

What had started as a would-be kidnapping somehow turned into Balor and I exchanging stories revolving around our clandestine "jobs." He shared countless accounts of mortals arriving in the Otherworld, not knowing they were dead or how they came to meet their demise. And I informed him of how gross it was when you've accidentally had puss splattered on your tongue after plunging a sword into a monster's chest cavity.

He'd even gone as far as feeding me. Considering he knew he couldn't poison me, I took the gesture as a sign of good faith. Plus—I was starving. Scooping the wooden bowl of beef stew into my still very shackled hands, I sipped from its rim.

Grá. I'm trying again.

And I hadn't stopped trying to call out to her. Every ten minutes, my tattoo reminded me. It wouldn't stop pestering me until I'd attempted as if some decorative ink had to remind me that my quite literal better half still wasn't within my godsdamned presence.

In between slurps, I shook the chain at Balor and mumbled, "Are these still necessary?"

"Very." Balor propped his chin on an elbow resting on the table. He crossed his legs and let out a bored sigh. "I stated I wished to talk with you, not that I trusted you, Druid."

Fair enough. Because I would have called on any and all elements within the rock walls littered with mossy patches around us to launch at his weaselly head.

"Alright." I set the bowl down and wiped my sleeve over my mouth. "Neither of us is getting any younger, so let's talk."

Balor tapped a pale finger against his temple. "As much as I hate to admit it, we both share the same thorn in our sides."

Pausing mid-slurp, I arched a brow at him over the bowl. "Tell me you're not referring to Dully?"

"One in the same."

It didn't make one lick of sense, but if I heard correctly, this could fare greatly in our favor.

I abandoned my stew on the table before pointing a finger at Balor. "So, you're telling me you're *not* all chummy with the Dullahan? With Crom?"

"Once upon a time, perhaps." Balor didn't make eye contact with me and flicked a dead worm from his fingernail. "But that was long before Lugh killed me. Second chances tend to put things in perspective." He stroked a finger over the metal plate where his once destructive third eye used to be. "Something I'm certain your dear Abigail could agree on."

Her name falling from the serpent's tongue had me pulling the cuff chain taut. The tattoo burned, itched, pulsed beneath my sleeve. "Don't you dare say her name."

"I can, and I will." Balor uncrossed his leg and pressed his forearms to the table, bringing our faces close enough I could head butt him but, for whatever reason—didn't. "She is the sole reason this entire plan will work. That is if you're not stupid enough to deny me."

My grip on the chain hadn't loosened.

"I'm listening."

The entrance door burst open, sending spires of wooden splinters dashing in every direction. Balor all but ducked under the table, and I held my arms above my head, her scent the only thing keeping me from tackling her to the ground. The raven flew in behind her as some form of aerial counterattack, cawing and flapping its wings, making laps around the room.

"Abby, grá, it's me," I shouted from behind my fleshy arm shield.

Abby stood with the dagger I'd made for her raised above her head, ready to stab Balor as many times as it took for her to feel better.

"Of course, I know it's you, Erimon. I'm here to force Balor to let you go so we can go find the others." Abby inched forward, peering at Balor as he rose from underneath the table and adjusted his shirt.

Rising, I moved toward her with lifted cuffed palms. "I'd

rather you not skewer him just yet, if you don't mind. This—" I jangled the shackles. "—isn't what it looks like."

"It isn't?" Abby dropped her eyes to the chain before shifting her attention back to Balor. "Because what it looks like, grá, is Balor kidnapped you and is stalling for the Dullahan."

My fair maiden knight and the fiery glow I could sense radiating underneath her jacket. What I wouldn't have given centuries ago to know that this woman was to be my mate.

"Abby, I know this sounds daft, but Balor wants to *help* us with Dully."

Abby's eyes narrowed into slits, and she brandished the blade in her grasp.

"Miss Weber, you're just in time to hear my proposal. Why don't you put the weapon away, take a seat, and have a listen? Hm?" Balor, cool as a snow-capped mountain, gestured toward the empty chair.

"Or—" Abby kicked the chair away from the table. "—I *keep* the dagger where it is, and you remove Erimon's cuffs. Because the way I see it, whatever your plan entails, there's something big in it for you, so if you want us to hear you out, you'll do as I damn well ask."

If only the threat of the Dullahan hadn't hung so heavy in the air, or I had the power to make Balor vanish. Because I was ready to bend her over the table and fuck her brains out for her ferocious browbeating.

Adjusting my trousers, I lifted the shackles toward Balor with a wicked grin, knowing he couldn't deny her.

Balor's cheek twitched before he fanned his fingers. The shackles fell in a lifeless heap on the table with a loud metallic *pang.* I rubbed my wrists and sat backward on the chair, resting my arms cooly on the back of it.

"There. Happy?" Balor impatiently drummed his fingers on the table.

Abby kept the dagger trained on Balor and sat, scooting her chair closer to me until our thighs touched. The raven landed on her shoulder and folded its wings back. "I'd be happier if the Dullahan wasn't a continuing problem. What's your plan?"

Balor steepled his fingers. "The source of Crom's power lies within the glowing head you've seen dangling from his steed. But it's a mirage. You see a human skull, a deterrent to keep most from tampering with it. In reality—" Balor poked the middle of his chest. "It's his *soul.*"

Abby and I shifted in our seats, alerting to attention, but still playing it cool.

"All we have to do is steal the head?" I asked, shrugging.

It sounded far too simple.

"It isn't that simple," Balor countered.

And I'd spoken too soon.

Abby rubbed her thumb over the Celtic engravings of her blade's hilt, not speaking, but waiting for Balor to continue.

"Crom, for good reason, guards that thing with his life. So does his loyal horse, and to make it worse, an enchantment must be used to counteract and remove it from the bridle." Balor rubbed his chin as if he'd only gotten this far in his scheme.

"And do you know how to counteract the enchantment?" Abby asked.

Balor shook his head and let out a gruff sigh. "No. That's not within my power. Do you all have someone within your merry band proficient with spells or curses?"

Edging closer to Abby, I let her tantalizing scent calm my senses. "Morrigan or Rhiannon?"

"Morrigan." Balor blew out a breath, his eyes widening as if genuinely surprised. "Yes. She'll be more than capable. Have her main focus be on that head. Once she lifts the enchantment, I can use his trust in me to get close enough to retrieve it."

Abby's weapon lowered with each passing second until it rested limply in her grasp, her knuckles grazing the table. "And after it's detached?"

"Then the rest is up to you, my dear. You *are* the key. But the how of it, I couldn't tell you. That's something you'll need to figure out on your own." Balor rubbed his thumb and forefinger together, tilting his head to one side, examining my beloved mate.

It was a stare two seconds too long for comfort, and a possessive growl gathered in the back of my throat.

Balor snapped me a feral glare. "Calm down, Druid. I have no interest in your pet."

Abby slammed the blade into the table, tapping her fingernail on the hilt and shutting us both right the fuck up. "And what's in this for you, Balor? Think we'll do this without knowing?"

"Of course not. I'd have been disappointed if you didn't ask." Balor stood and re-buttoned his cufflinks to his sleeves. "I want full power back. The way it used to be. The way it should be. I don't need Crom's assistance any longer."

Feeling fidgety, I opened and closed my hand, pulling wooden shards from the table only to repeatedly settle them back into place. "And you're willing to throw away your friendship for power?"

"Friendship?" Balor chuckled and looked to the cave ceiling. "Hardly. We've never been more than acquaintances, really."

"Does Crom know that?" Abby's voice sounded a bit melancholy like she felt remorse for her would-be killer.

"It's of no consequence." Balor pressed his fingertips to the table and glanced from Abby to me. "Now then. Do we have a deal, Druids?"

What's your take, Abby?

I don't like it one bit, but it's the best chance we've got.

Agreed.

"How can we trust you won't back out on this plan at the last second?" Abby so wisely asked, her knuckles stroking the raven's feathers.

"I'd imagine you can't trust me. But what choice do you have? Let's say I did betray you and didn't uphold my end of the bargain. Well, then, you'd be in the same position to defeat him as you were before I offered you this deal. Wouldn't you?" Balor arched a brow and impatiently beat his finger against the wood. "Deal. Or no deal? Time is fleeting."

Rising, after exchanging one final determined glance, Abby and I extended our hands. With a serpent's grin, Balor shook them both before striding for the door.

"I will now go and keep up appearances. You must hurry to find the rest of your group before the full moon settles." Balor reached for the door handle.

"You're not going to tell us where they are?" I threw my arms out at my sides.

Balor smirked and whipped the door open. "No."

Giving another blood-curdling cackle, Balor disappeared into the darkness.

Abby curled her arm with mine and sighed. "I hope we made the right decision, Mon."

"Mon?" Offering a lopsided smile, I bumped my knuckle under her chin. "I don't recall you ever calling me that."

Abby turned to face me, flipping my hand over and tracing the lines and grooves of my palm. "I'm serious. We can't trust him."

"You're right. We can't. But know what we can trust?" I tugged her close until her chest pressed to my ribs. "Our bond. Our friends. And we can also trust that Balor wants that ultimate power. He won't back out on this Abby. He won't."

Abby wrapped her arms around my neck, and after pressing a silky kiss to my lips, said, "Let's go collect our family."

19

ABBY

WITH OUR HANDS ENTWINED, ERIMON and I ventured into the darkness again in search of the group. There was no telling how we would find them without the kind of connection Erimon and I had, but even the never-ending loop this place appeared to be must have a beginning and end.

"So, I was shacking it up with Balor in a pair of magical cuffs. Where were you all the while?" Erimon bumped his shoulder against mine, giving me that sultry grin that never failed to make my stomach flutter.

I stopped walking because gathering my thoughts over everything Vesta had told me took so much focus, I couldn't do anything else. Squeezing Erimon's hand, I turned to face him and took a deep, soothing breath before speaking. "The first Bandruí visited me. Her spirit did. I think?"

Erimon's sky-blue eyes flickered, and he appeared somewhat taken aback. "Yeah? What'd she have to say?"

"She knew everything. That my birth was a clandestine plan.

You and I were destined to unite to end the Dullahan's cycle. She said she sparked a deal with the Elder, that his duty was to ensure destiny put you on the right path to find me." I tilted my head to one side, hoping to catch his initial reaction to this.

A charming playfulness danced in Erimon's gaze before it spread to his radiant grin. "And that's why he was such a crotchety old fart to me. He wanted to uphold his end of the bargain, but I was being a stubborn jackass at every turn."

Chuckling, but tears forming in my eyes, I said, "Or maybe it was just because you were such a brat overall."

Erimon joined in laughing with me at first until he blinked at a tear rolling down my cheek. He swished it away with his finger and pulled me closer. "Hey now. Why are you cryin', grá?"

"She told me something else, Mon." Hesitance stole the words from my throat at first, a strangled lump forming there, and I coughed.

Erimon grabbed my shoulders. "Abby, are you alright?"

After getting it together, I nodded, clearing my throat several times until I could speak. "She knew who my parents were. Their names. My mother was human and my father—" I lifted my gaze to meet my Druid's eyes, hesitant to admit it at first. "—he was *fae*."

Erimon didn't look as disgusted as I thought he'd be. In fact, I'd dare say he looked—delighted.

"That's amazing. Why do you look disappointed?" Erimon traced a finger over my jawline.

"Because I thought you *would* be. I seem to recall when we first met, you said something about you never getting along with them. And now I'm here standing as half of one." I flail my hands over half my body, displaying myself.

Erimon hung his head low, shaking it before massaging between my shoulder blades and up the back of my neck. "I give the fae shite because I poke fun at their lifestyle and the way they came about, but that's all it is, Abby. Jokes. Clearly, I was wrong because I most certainly get along with *you* superbly, right?" He kissed my cheek, and the subtleness of his lips caressing my skin made my knees wobbly. "It *is* amazin'. Truly. It explains a lot about your untapped power," Erimon added.

Nodding, even though I still couldn't comprehend it all, I sighed. "I know it's selfish, but I wish I knew more. If what everyone keeps saying is true, that I'm destined for all these things, then why would the universe take my parents from me? The Elder made it sound like they were merely breeders, and once I was born, the world no longer needed them and it discarded them."

I needed them.

Nausea rose in my stomach and I pressed a hand there to calm it.

Erimon slipped his palm over it and shook his head. "Firstly, it's not selfish. Why wouldn't anyone want to know more about their parents? And secondly, I highly doubt your ma and da were simply thrown away. There had to be a reason for them leaving this earth."

A cloud of inky tendrils with a duo of crows emerged from the darkness, causing Emrys to flare his wings wide and squawk in defense. Erimon sprung his own wings out, our stances both changing to attack, before a female body formed, tripping and toppling. Morrigan hopped to her feet, straightening her disheveled hair and coughing through the smoke that lingered from her apparent botched teleport.

She blew rogue strands of dark tendrils from her eyes and wrapped her arms around me in a *hug*. "I can honestly say I'm ever so delighted to see you."

Glancing at Erimon for an answer to her strange behavior proved useless, and I awkwardly patted Morrigan's back. "I'm glad to see you too, Morrigan. Are you—alright?"

Erimon arched a brow at my feeble attempt at compassion, and I widened my eyes at him. I'd never been great at empathizing with people. Animals were an entirely different story, but humans were always a struggle.

"I went through the Wave as my crows, and I haven't been able to shift back until coming in contact with you both." Morrigan stared into the distance behind me, her grip on my shoulders tightening enough to make me wince. "I've been flying in darkness for—" Her dark gaze lifted to meet mine, the confusion and vulnerability playing in it, reminding me of a lost child. "—how long have we been here?"

Patting her arm to grab her attention, I softened my eyes. "A few hours. Did you come across anything or anyone strange?"

Morrigan coughed, cleared her throat, and fanned her palms down the front of her robes. "No. There was nothing but the sounds of distant whispers that I couldn't decipher. Otherwise, pure bleedin' darkness. It takes a lot to make me uneasy." She glanced around and shivered. "I suppose the Otherworld would be the thing to do it."

Still settled on my shoulder, Emrys squawked at Morrigan, and she sneered at him.

"We've got to find the others. I've lost all sense of time here, and the full moon could be approaching at any moment." Erimon held his hand out to me.

I wanted nothing more than to ask Morrigan if she could see anything from my past regarding my parents using her magical sight. Not only had I not felt right asking for a favor that paled compared to the one she was about to do, but this wasn't the time or place for it.

"Any thoughts on how we're supposed to find the others?" Frowning, I squeezed Erimon's hand. "We barely found each other and have an eternal *bond*."

Morrigan brushed past us, snapping her fingers, and making small plumes of smoke and feathers waft from her hand. "That should be—" Snarling, she snapped a final time with more fervor and ignited a fireball in her palm. "—a lot easier than trying to find *you* two."

"Are you forgetting I'm a Bandruí?" I held out my hand to Morrigan, easily producing a bouncing flame.

Morrigan only gave it a glance before shrugging. "Not at all. I've just always been the sort not to rely on others easily."

"Well, Phantom Queen, we have little choice but to rely on you at his point. You say it's easy to locate them all?" Erimon waved his arm forward, encouraging her to take the lead. "Then, by all means—*find* them."

"Correction. I said it was easier. Emphasis on the 'er,' but it's of no matter. Your bond drew me to you. It gives off such a vibrant tone that it made it's nearly impossible to ignore, and I didn't know what was pulling me." Morrigan worked her way through the stone corridors with us trailing on her heels. "My only thought was that I prayed it wasn't something leading me to my death."

"And why wouldn't they all think the same thing and resist the celestial pull?" Erimon asked.

Morrigan halted and turned from left to right, deciding on a direction. "Oh, they'll most certainly try, but as I said, it's impossible to ignore. If my gut instincts are correct, I'd say we run into Rhiannon first."

"Because she's so optimistic and light-hearted?" I guessed.

Morrigan swiped her hand over something wet and glistening from the nearby rock wall. She ran it between two fingers and smelled it. "Hm. Only water. And no, it's because she's naïve and wistful."

Erimon scoffed. "More naïve than the Chaun?"

Morrigan whipped around to face us, making us stumble so we narrowly avoided stepping on her toes. "The goddess who insists on bringing her unicorn wherever she goes like it's a domesticated house cat?"

"I see your point," Erimon mumbled, rubbing his thumb under his jawline and making his brow bob with a hurry-up expression.

Morrigan ran the finger that'd touched the wall, still moist, over her bottom lip. "There has to be more to pulse the enchanting pull to them all like a damned beacon." Gasping, she tugged at our jackets, grimacing when they weren't coming off fast enough to her liking.

"Mor?" Erimon arched his brow. "If this is your way of askin' for a ménage à trois, now is hardly the time."

Morrigan's expression fell unamused, and her hands went

limp at her sides. "Honestly, is everything about sex with you, Druid?"

"Yes," we replied in unison.

The lustful side gaze Erimon shot my way had my core and cheeks on fire.

Morrigan pinched the bridge of her nose. "The frenzy of fresh mates. Look, can you two just make your tattoos do that glowing thing they do? It may help strengthen the signal, so to speak."

I frowned at the way she'd said that. As if the ravenous, unquenching thirst I felt for Erimon, the need for him, was a passing fancy. Like what we shared was akin to puppy love and destined to fizzle out.

Don't go letting Morrigan in your head, grá. No two pairings are the same. I'll happily screw you until neither of us can walk every single night for the rest of eternity.

As we slipped off our jackets, I had to bite away the smile tickling my lips from Erimon's naughty thought. We turned to each other, Morrigan becoming a blurred background to our center stage. Our jackets fell to our feet, and Erimon wrapped an arm around my waist, pulling me flush against him and pressing a hand on my tailbone. Emrys flapped his wings, cawing and diving to the ground. Our arms brushed, the static shock of skin-to-skin contact giving us glorious goosebumps. Granting Morrigan's wish, the tattoos brightened with swirling tendrils of sapphire and ruby.

I don't understand how anyone could ever grow tired of this.

I'd projected the thought to him, letting my eyes do the smiling that begged at my lips.

And what is this, *Abby?*

This tenderhearted concern for another's well-being. Someone who once was a stranger but now is the most familiar person in the universe. This immense affection. And the swell that forms in your chest when either one calls the other mine.

An untamed urge swirled in Erimon's sky-blue gaze before his mouth crashed against mine. Morrigan hadn't asked for it, and Elders only knew if she was even still in the same space as us. But Erimon poured every ache, regret, and promise to come into that kiss. I levitated from Erimon lifting us from the ground with his wings, turning us in a languid circle as our lips devoured each other. A kiss may simply be another form of affection to most, but for me, it was the source of life and a symbol of everything Erimon had and is still willing to give me—to bestow upon his *mate*.

"For cryin' out loud. How long have they been like that?" Finn's deep, rumbly voice echoed in my mind.

Slowly pulling away, I stared at Erimon in a euphoric haze. "Did I hear Finn, or was that a hallucination?"

"I better damn well not be a fever dream, or we're all *really* in some shite," Finn barked.

Grinning, my cheeks blushing with warmth, I pressed my forehead to Erimon's, and he lowered me back to solid ground. They were all there *staring* at us. Between when our tattoos did their color dance and we'd gotten lost in each other's thoughts and that cosmically numbing kiss, they'd all find their way to us.

"Told you it'd work. The kiss was a nice touch, too." Morrigan smirked.

Cu folded his arms with a huff. "Can we go kill the Dullahan now so I never have to see these two swappin' spit again?"

"You sound jealous," Mave said, flashing Cu a wicked grin.

Cu waved her off. "Of mates? I don't need some universal fated pull to bed a woman of *any* variety, Cow Queen."

"Even pixies?" Rhiannon genuinely asked, blinking at Cu with astute curiousness.

Cu's confidence dwindled slightly, his taut arms relaxing. "Well, I don't know about all that."

Patrick bounced on his heels and raised a finger. "Oh, what about trolls?"

Cu grimaced and uncrossed his arms. "Alright, alright. Are we going to stop this chaos cycle or not?"

"You're only so fortunate that the full moon is moments away, hound." Morrigan clasped her hands under her chin and grinned. "Because I do so enjoy seeing you in an entirely different form of spasm."

Cu took several steps toward Morrigan, his gigantic hands forming fists. Mave stuck the blade of her sword in his way, and he stopped, glaring first at the weapon and then at the Warrior Queen.

The stone floor beneath us rumbled, cracks forming in the walls, producing billowing smoke and raging flames. The steady suddenness of a horse's hooves galloping in the distance grew nearer and nearer until a gateway to what appeared as hell itself opened in front of us. There, seated upon his midnight steed, his face shadowed in a torn grey cloak, was the Dullahan. And, resting at his side, hanging from its usual place off the bridle, was the head—the Dullahan's *soul.*

20

ERIMON

THIS WAS IT. ABBY AND I had come together as the universe desired. We accepted our bond, became eternal mates, and Abby gained her Bandruí powers through transference and re-birth. All that was left was to stop the cycle of chaos, and we'll have upheld our side of the bargain. Was it so much to hope, to pray, that would be all that eternity asked of us for a *very* long time? Could we finally just be Abigail and Erimon without hellspawn dogs, goblins, or death gods leaping from the shadows at every corner?

Though, I wasn't sure how long we would last through a calm existence. Neither of us was born to lead a normal life. The universe hadn't given us such immense power to have it wasted playing house in a cottage nestled deeply within the forest with an animal farm and crops. But a Druid could dream. And maybe, just possibly, if eons from now, *I* would become an Elder, perhaps we could have those things. For now, with my mate at my side, our mission was to stop the

Dullahan and take over the thrones for High King and Queen. All in a Druid day's work.

I know I have no reason to ask this, but still will because I care about you. Are you ready for this, grá?

Despite the looming terror of the Dullahan approaching, Abby leaned toward me, pressed a soft kiss to my cheek, and blessed me with a reassuring, radiant smile.

I'm ready to get this over with and become your Queen, Druid.

If I needed any more incentive to ensure this battle ended as quickly as possible, that was it. I only prayed to the Elders that Balor kept his word and didn't stab us in the back. Let his growing lust for overwhelming power keep him an honest death god.

And speaking of the Devil…

Balor appeared from behind the Dullahan's massive steed, his palms pressed together, and that wicked glint in his gaze that always made the hairs on the back of my neck stand up.

"Tell me. How does it feel to know this will be the last day you all walk this earth after thousands of years between you?" Balor shifted his eyes from one companion to the other, but no one responded to his outrageous question.

The Dullahan snapped his reins and lifted a bony finger aimed at Abby. "Enough of this. Your essence *will* be mine tonight, Abigail Weber. Immortal or not, it is still *mine* to claim."

Abby, my mate, my fated bond, slid a foot forward with the confidence of a lioness on the prowl and raised her hand, igniting a fireball within it. "You have your words, Crom. While I have an *army*."

More truer words couldn't have been spoken. Abby had us

all at her back from the day she waltzed into our lives, and we knew without explanation that she was something special—someone to be protected.

Cu was already halfway through transforming into his warm-spasm form, and Finn lifted the empty hilt, dragging his hand down the length to make the fog blade appear. Mave removed the massive sword from the sheath at her back and gave it a single twirl. Patrick beat his fists together, the liquid gold pooling over his hands and knuckles hardening. A glittering, silver helmet appeared over Rhiannon's unicorn's head, its horn protruding from the center. Rhiannon waved her hand over the creature's back, producing an opal white saddle, which she sat on proudly. Morrigan splayed her hand at her side, conjuring the lethal spear with a titanium blade she'd often wield in battle.

I stepped behind my Bandruí, pressing a palm to the small of her back while pulling bits of rock and sand from the surrounding ground and walls. It formed levitating projectiles ready to launch into the Dullahan's skull.

The Dullahan roared, rattling the stonewalls and making pebbles and debris fall. The horse charged toward us, Abby throwing one, two, and even three fireballs like she'd been wielding that power for years instead of days. Rhiannon's unicorn cut in front of us, galloping at the approaching equine creature. Rhiannon produced a silver shield and raised it to just below her nose. The unicorn ducked its head, aiming the sharpened horn at the horse's body. It was like a lance striking a solid chunk of meat when they collided.

The Dullahan's horse whinnied and lost its footing but

quickly regained composure and continued its antagonizing gallop. Rhiannon turned the unicorn around, ready to strike again from the side. While I launched continued arrows made of sand and rock in the Dullahan's direction, I kept a keen eye on Balor. He fought Finn, meeting him blow for blow with his iron sword, but made no signs of the plan we'd discussed earlier. That was until his gaze cut to the head swinging erratically from the Dullahan's saddle.

Balor looks like he's still in on the plan. Keep fighting and wait for him to give a signal.

Abby slapped her palms together and yanked her hands out to the sides, producing a taut line of fire that she hurled toward Dully. He ducked, but the blow singed the top part of his hood.

Signal? What kind of signal? Wasn't that something we should've discussed earlier?

Damn it all to Dubnos.

Taking out my frustration, I thrust my hands upward, sending sharp spikes of hardened sand to the horse's front, right, and left. The annoying bugger avoided every fucking one of them too.

Probably. But he sort of left without giving us much detail.

Cu stormed past us with his slow but powerful gait vibrating the rock flooring beneath our boots. He swung his massive arms several times, missing the mark, but on the fifth swing, his hand slammed into the side of the horse, sending both it and the Dullahan flying into the nearest wall.

The Dullahan has been separated from his horse.

The excited tone in Abby's voice was enough to make my

heart gallop faster than Rhiannon's unicorn as it headed for the rattled death steed. There was so much hope and pleading in that singular thought from my mate that it throttled me into a crazed defense.

Dullahan, now standing vulnerable on his feet, did *not* go unnoticed by Balor. He kept Finn busy in an epic battle of swordplay that could very well continue for a millennium if neither bothered to stop it.

While I kept near Abby's side, Morrigan charged at the Dullahan, Patrick flanking from the other direction. Morrigan thrust her spear at the Dullahan's ribs, but he snapped his spine whip around it, locking her weapon in place. Patrick beat his solid gold fists repeatedly against Dully's shoulders and back, but the strength the death god had gained since our last fight made Patrick's punches appear like he had been punching with pillows instead of solid metallic limbs. With his free hand, Dully shoved his palm into Patrick's chest, sending him flailing to the other side of the space in a cart-wheeling spiral.

Mave's eyes widened to the size of saucers. "Patrick," she cried out, running to his aid.

The Dullahan's horse continued to gallop as if it knew the prized possession it carried and wouldn't stop for anything to protect its master. Dully attempted to pull Morrigan toward him with the whip tightly wrapping her spear, but she wound her arm around the hilt, twisting and yanking until the weapon was free. Using the blunt side, she slammed it into the ground like a pole vault and launched herself, landing at the Dullahan's feet.

"Rhiannon," I barked, waiting for her to turn her attention

to me. "Focus on the horse. Use that unicorn of yours to stop it. Whatever you need to do."

Rhiannon blinked her bright eyes at me, not acting at first.

"That's an order," I roared, furrowing my brow and pointing at the still-wandering death horse.

Rhiannon emphatically nodded before clipping her heels at the unicorn's sides, chasing after the other horse as it galloped laps around everyone. Balor made eye contact with me long enough to give a solid and affirming nod.

Patrick groaned, his hands having morphed back to normal, and he held his head as Mave helped him to sit up. "A lot of good I'm doing. I can't even put a dent in him."

"Stay here or try to help Rhiannon stop the horse," Mave said cooly, slapping Patrick on the back to get him to move.

"The horse? And you think *it's* not going to be any stronger than the Dullahan?" Patrick rubbed his neck and punched the air, calling on the golden metal to coat his arms again.

Mave twirled her sword and bumped her fist under Patrick's chin. "Only one way to find out, Chaun. And be careful. Phoebe would never forgive me if I brought you back unalive."

After flashing a dopey grin at the mention of Phoebe, Patrick sprinted after the horse, waving his arms and joining Rhiannon in attempting to stop it.

The Dullahan's whip circled and cut through the air above us, transporting me to chilling memories of that night he'd performed the same action. Only then, I'd had to watch the point of it lodge into Abby's chest. I'd had to stare in horror as blood soaked her shirt, her eyes wide and petrified. And I'd had to internally scream as the Dullahan yanked the whip from her breast, sending chunks of her flesh spraying as she fell in a lifeless heap to the floor.

It couldn't happen again. Ever.

Throwing my fist skyward, I caught the whip in mid-swing, Abby's hand landing next to mine. We peered at each other, both holding the Dullahan's weapon captive in our grasp. He tugged at it several times, but we held onto it far too steadily. The Dullahan may have grown stronger, but so had *we*—together.

Abby smiled at me, resplendent as the bone whip glowed a brightening orange until it caught fire. The flames kissed my knuckles as they traveled down the weapon's length, but it hadn't burned me because she *controlled* it. The fire continued until it reached the hilt, scorching the Dullahan's hands. He growled and stomped on the whip, breaking it in half, which also halted Abby's magic, but never let it go.

We were halfway there. We'd rid him of his ancient weapon, separated him from his horse, and—I'd always been one to speak far too damn soon.

The Dullahan snapped the half-destroyed whip, regrowing its missing length, the deadly point reforming itself. A chuckle rose deep within the death god's chest. The sheer patronizing sound of it was enough to catapult me, Abby, Mave, Morrigan, and Cu into blood-curdling action. We circled him, throwing anything and everything in our ethereal arsenals at him. Abby launched fireballs and raging flames; Mave slashed, poked, and struck with her sword, while Morrigan mirrored the same from the other side with her spear. Most of Cu's swings would miss, but when one landed, the Dullahan would rock on his feet, gain ground, and continue to bleedin' *laugh*.

I spiraled rock and sand together, throwing my opened palms at Dully's center, attempting to use the resources to carve a hole in his chest in the same spot he'd killed Abby. The Dullahan resisted it, and even though my arms shook, veins bulging in my neck and forehead, I kept pushing it into him bit by bit. I'd keep forcing it on him even if it took all damn night. He had to pay for what he did to my mate. The moment it happened before; I had no idea if I'd see her again. I wasn't certain what she was for *me*, and that realization only amplified my fury.

In the background, Balor had stopped fighting, leaving a very confused Finn scratching his head at his sudden surrender. Balor pointed at the horse and I snapped my attention to Morrigan.

"Morrigan, help with the horse," I shouted.

Morrigan scrunched her nose. "Me? Why? They have it handled." Grunting, she continued to prod Dully with her spear.

"*Now*, Mor."

After jabbing the death god a final time, she snarled under her breath, "Fine."

Balor gave me a subtle nod and I turned my attention back to the Dullahan before he caught wind of our exchange.

"When will you all realize that you cannot win? This is all pointless. The human might as well surrender to save you all the time, trouble, and quite possibly your *lives*," Dullahan spat behind the cowardice of his shadowed hood.

"I'm not human," Abby yelled, hurling a giant fireball. It was enough to catch the death god on fire and cause him a few seconds of pain, but not enough to end his miserable life.

The Dullahan's momentary wails of agony steadily flowed into maniacal cackling, and he spread his arms out to his sides. "As I told you from the very beginning. You *cannot* win."

"Crom," Balor beckoned.

Everyone aside from Abby and me turned to the would-be betrayer in unison. But we Druids remained focused on the Dullahan because we wanted to see his face—wished to bask in his reaction when he realized we *had* won.

"I believe I have something of yours," Balor added.

Shadows danced on the wall behind the Dullahan, figures of our companions standing motionless, but the one who stood out above them all raised an arm with something circular held within his grasp—the Dullahan's fucking *head*.

21

ABBY

BALOR KEPT HIS WORD—FOR now. This was still far from over, and something told me Crom wouldn't take Balor's betrayal lightly. If he'd been angry before, this would only make him *furious*.

"Balor, *what* are you doing?" Crom asked, his voice slightly cracking, and he wrung his hand on the whip's hilt.

Balor let out a mocking sigh, letting the decaying head fall slack in front of him, holding it by the few strands of long black hair still attached to the skull. "Let me start by saying this is truly nothing personal, old friend."

"Balor," Crom croaked, the name releasing from his throat like a chastising, threatening snarl.

Cu's hulking form started to stalk toward Balor, fully prepared to knock him into next Sunday, but Erimon threw his arm out, stopping him and shaking his head. Mave and Finn shared perplexed glances while Patrick caught my eye, shrugging with a "what gives" expression. I pressed a finger over my lips, hoping he'd take it as a cue that we'd explain it all later. Rhiannon squinted at the scene unfolding, her unicorn rearing to continue into battle, and she kept pulling on the reins to keep the creature at bay. Morrigan stepped away from the Dullahan's horse, dusting her hands of deep purple particles from whatever spell she cast to retrieve the head.

"There was a time when I ruled the Otherworld alone. I brought souls here from the surface, cast them to where they rightly belonged, and lived here as their fucking *King*." Lifting the head with a stiff arm, his eyes flashed with boiling rage. "Then the universe saw reason to create *you*. It was as if I needed to divide the tasks or wasn't upholding my duties even though I loved what I did. *Reveled* in it."

Crom wrapped his other hand around the whip, pulling it taut, his skeletal hands shaking. "The both of us overseeing death and the afterlife was fated. Your death, too, was fated. What are you trying to do here, Balor?"

Balor lowered the head and stroked the top with a single thin finger, a smile creeping at the corner of his lips. "Morrigan, my dear. Would you be a gem and enlighten Crom about *fate*?"

Morrigan didn't budge initially, her eyes turning on Erimon for approval beforehand. When he gave her the nod, she flipped her crimson robes behind her and moved next to Balor. Morrigan held her palms out, facing them upward. A glowing pentagram appeared on her skin on one hand, the Celtic infinity symbol in the other. Her eyes turned a smoky white, and her head dipped backward.

Cu had reverted to his more human-looking form and rubbed the back of his neck, looking away from Morrigan. "I bleedin' hate when she does this."

"It's rather poetic if you ask me," Mave countered, leaning on her sword's hilt, the point of the blade digging into the sand.

"You *would* say that," Cu grumbled.

Several beats passed before Morrigan closed her hands, lifted her head, and the symbols disappeared from her palms. "You've fulfilled your destiny, Crom. The Dullahan was initially created as a symbol and counter to Balor's needed demise. The time has come for a new cycle to begin, and you—" Morrigan methodically shook her head left to right. "—aren't part of it."

Balor roared with laughter, the head bouncing within his grasp. "Don't you see, Crom? You've been written out. You were supposed to mark Abigail and become obsessed with claiming her essence. Because *that* is what set up this entire scene. It was all to lead *right* here."

And here I was, somehow feeling *remorse* for the creature who killed me once and sought to do it again. They made it sound like he couldn't physically *do* anything else. His marks were his existence, and that he wasn't *allowed* to deviate from his fate.

"You will regret this one day." Crom stayed eerily still, the only motion coming from the imaginary breeze flapping his tattered cloak.

His black horse puffed smoke and fire from its nostrils, scraping its hooves against the ground, representing his master's growing anger.

"I somehow doubt that. Consider our partnership—" Balor snapped his fingers, and the Dullahan's horse turned to mist and smoke that floated into nothingness, its distant whinnies fading until it was gone. "—terminated."

I feel sick, Erimon. This doesn't seem right.

Erimon curved his arm around my waist.

The lesser of two evils, grá. None of it is meant to feel right.

"No," Crom bellowed, extending a hand toward the barren space where his horse had been.

Balor picked lint from his lapels, flicking it. "Now, you know I don't get my hands dirty. But these folks? They're rearing for revenge for the grief you caused them. And I'm going to step out of their way."

The Dullahan hunched forward, swirling the whip above his head and cracking it. "You cannot kill me."

"Perhaps not." Balor began to move backward. "But they're certainly going to try."

"Erimon," I said, already forming a fireball in my palm. "This would be the other part of the plan Balor was vague about."

Erimon squeezed my hip before spinning toward a subtlety retreating Balor. "Balor, how are we supposed to finish this?"

Cackling, Balor shrugged. "I have no idea. But I've done my part. The rest—" He tossed the head to me, and I juggled with it, almost catching it on fire until I was able to get a grip on one half-decayed ear. "—is up to you."

With a final echoing laugh, Balor disappeared into the darkness, leaving us with a very pissed-off former death god.

Gagging at the putrid smell of the decaying head nestled in the crook of my arm, I nudged Erimon. "What the *hell* am I supposed to do with this?"

"I don't know. Go to Morrigan. She must know something." Erimon pulled me toward him with his hand on the back of my neck and kissed me. "I wanted you to train with your

Druid powers first, but it would seem the Bandruí needs the spotlight, Abby." He traced his thumb over my cheek. "Go talk to her. And whatever you do, do *not* let him get that head."

Nodding, I held the skull with both arms like a running back in football and sprinted to Morrigan.

"Everyone," Erimon announced, sliding the jacket from his shoulders and throwing it aside. "Keep Dully away from Abby. And this time, I fucking *mean* it." He flared his wings, poising them behind him for attack.

"With pleasure," Cu growled, curling his shoulders forward and forcing his warm-spasm transformation.

The Dullahan swung his whip as Erimon, Cu, and Finn attacked first, slashing, punching, shoving, and kicking. Patrick slapped his face several times before invoking his golden fists and running toward the dogpile with a shrill battle cry.

Morrigan motioned me to a corner and crouched to one knee. "I'm going to need you to learn quickly, Abby. Do you understand me?"

"Learn? What do you mean? What do I have to do?" I didn't let go of the head for anything, clinging it against my stomach as if it were my source of life. In some warped sense, it really was.

Grunts, hollers, and yells came from behind us. Erimon leapt onto Dullahan's back, trying to pry his hood off.

Morrigan slipped the cloak's hood over her head and thinned her lips. "The only thing Crom said correctly was that we cannot kill him."

My stomach bottomed out and my throat tightened. "What do you mean we can't *kill* him? Wasn't that my entire purpose for existing? To destroy him?"

Finn roared and stormed at Dullahan with his fog sword raised high. Patrick kept getting thrown several meters away but would simply shake his head, beat his fists together, and consistently rejoin the fight.

"My dear," Morrigan started, pressing a cool palm to my heated cheek. "Don't reduce yourself to such a singular purpose. This is one of many destinies you've yet to live. Trust me."

Previously, I'd only ever seen mischief and mirth play in Morrigan's gaze, but the way she looked at me now with such conviction, I couldn't help but believe her.

"He's trying to run away," Mave shouted.

Cu's gigantic form stomped behind us. "No, he won't." Cu tackled him to the ground, Finn and Erimon piling over him to hold Dullahan down.

"Then what do I need to do, Mor?" I locked eyes with the Celtic goddess, ensuring she knew I was ready to do whatever it took.

Morrigan began to roll up her sleeves. "We can't kill him, but we can ensnare him in a fleshy shell. He'll retain some of his powers because he's always possessed them, but he'll essentially be a demi-god."

The chaos cycle will cease.

"How do we do it?" I glanced at our counterparts, still tackling, slashing, and punching the Dullahan to keep him away from us.

Erimon stood, his wings' feathers rustling, and he cracked his neck to one side. He dove onto Crom again with his shoulder, flattening him to the ground.

"First, face me and set the head on the ground between us."

Morrigan stood slightly to my right and pointed at our feet.

As if protecting a child, I turned my torso away with the head cradled in my arm and frowned at her. "That'll make it accessible to him. We can't let him have it."

Morrigan placed a gentle hand on my arm and coaxed my grip away from the head, gesturing for me to give it to her. "Do you honestly think those five will let him anywhere near this thing after all they've been through? Besides, what we're about to invoke, there's not a chance in the cosmos he'll be able to get close."

I nodded and placed the head on the ground as instructed.

"Now, Abby, listen to me." Morrigan grabbed my biceps and garnered my attention. "To do this, we're going to invoke the Rule of Three. That requires three witches—a triangle. But the point must be the most powerful."

Surely, she meant herself.

"You? Right? You're a *goddess*, Morrigan."

Morrigan slowly shook her head before poking my shoulder. "No. I'm a goddess of fate and war with witch-like power. *You* are a Bandruí. You must serve as the point."

Unease, fear, and overwhelming worry for my friends' lives consumed me. Terror for my *mate's* life.

"I can't. I've barely learned how to control my Druid fire magic. I've yet to even tap into my Bandruí side. How am I supposed—"

Morrigan cut me off by slapping a hand over my mouth. "Stop it. You're going to listen to me and do as I say. You *can* do this. It's in your blood and only needs to be coaxed out. You *will* do this because you know what can happen if you *don't*."

She nudged her chin toward the group still fighting Dullahan.

Patrick's breaths had become labored, his swings slower, yet he still tried. Mave's hair was disheveled, the sword heavier in her grasp, but when she screamed her war cry to the skies, it gave her a second wind. Cu stumbled, using a stone wall to steady himself, his warp-spasm fading. He sucked in several quick breaths before continuing his fist barrage in his smaller form. Finn blocked the lashes of Dullahan's spine whip with his fog sword, several pieces of his tunic ripped to shreds from the whip's sharp points. And Erimon, my mate, my Druid, his bronzed chest glistening with sweat and his majestic wings, stopped for nothing despite me being able to sense his growing exhaustion.

There was a moment when time seemed to slow, and Erimon's ice-blue eyes found mine. Despite how tired he was and the growing urgency of our situation, he gave me one of his trademark smiles.

You can do this, Abby. Do it for you. Do it for our bond. And do it for family.

My sinuses stung, and I whipped my attention back to Morrigan. "Tell me what to do. Wait. There's only two of us."

"Rhiannon," Morrigan called out. "We need you. And *leave* the unicorn."

Rhiannon blinked confusedly but dismounted her steed, petted its muzzle, and joined us. "What's going on?"

"We need your power. We'll invoke the Rule of Three to banish Crom using *that*." Morrigan pointed at the gnarled head on the ground, the cavity where an eye was staring at us.

Rhiannon grimaced from the stench and covered her nose with the back of her hand. "It's been ages since I've done the Rule."

"Yeah? It's Abby's first time, and she's the point, so I'm sure you'll do just fine, Rhian." Morrigan yanked Rhiannon beside her.

"Her *first* time?" Rhiannon stared at Morrigan with wide eyes, her tone nowhere near reassuring.

"Not helping," Morrigan spat through gritted teeth.

"What do I *do*, Mor?" My words were rushed and impatient.

Morrigan slid two fingers down her exposed forearm, revealing glowing runes and words I hadn't recognized. "I'm going to tell you the incantation words you'll say, and I need you to put them to memory because your voice must be the loudest. Do you understand?"

"Yes."

Morrigan read the symbols from her skin, and not only did I listen to her with piqued ears, but I watched her mouth form the syllables, her tongue moving to her teeth during the parts with lilts and accented letters, and the way her throat bobbed between words.

"Do you have all that?" Morrigan asked, tilting her head to one side to read my expression.

The incantation floated through my brain like it'd been there for decades despite having only heard it once. "Yes."

"Good. Because I don't have time to repeat it."

"How the fuck is he crawling with us on top of him?" Mave shouted.

I peered over my shoulder to find Crom slithering on the ground inch by inch toward me with Mave, Finn, and Cu sitting on top of him.

Morrigan grabbed my chin and turned my face back to hers. "Don't let it distract you. You *must* concentrate, Abby."

Easier said than done with the Dullahan creeping toward my heels behind me, but I nodded at her.

"When you say the words, call to your power, even if it's the Druid power at first," Morrigan started.

"My Druid powers? It could *burn* you both." The thought of it had me stepping backward, but Morrigan latched onto my hand, gripping it—hard.

"It can't hurt us. Not while we're connected." Morrigan grabbed Rhiannon's hand and motioned for her to take my other free one.

The three of us stood in a triangle with me as the point, the Dullahan's soul resting on the ground between us. When we'd formed the physical connection, runes, symbols, and script glowed from most of Morrigan's exposed flesh. My tattoo shimmered and sizzled underneath my jacket, and Rhiannon's hair gained a radiant glow as if the sun had blessed it.

Closing my eyes, I recited the incantation, and Morrigan and Rhiannon spoke in tandem with me. It was neither wholly Gaelic nor a language I recognized but something entirely its own.

We repeated it several times, the untapped Bandruí power that had lain dormant within my veins, punching at my skin, yearning to be free. An ache formed in my temple, and I opened my heart to it, opened my soul, and my mated bond to it. A surge shot through my chest, traveling up my neck and circling in my mind until I gasped. The only thing that kept me from crying out and collapsing to my knees was the hands I held of my fellow witches. Their power gave me the strength to push through it and unleash everything in my true potential.

"No," Crom roared, his wails echoing off the cave walls.

Mallacht.

Mallacht.

Mallacht.

I opened my eyes just as the world and my vision fell into complete darkness.

22

ERIMON

IT HAD ALL HAPPENED SO quickly. In one instant, Balor betrayed Crom, giving us the golden opportunity to finally stop him. In another, Abby ran off to chase her Bandruí destiny, and I and my heroic counterparts did everything we could to delay the Dullahan. We punched, kicked, stabbed, clawed, and piled on him like bags of flour, all until our ethereal buckets were beyond empty, but still, we pressed on even while running on fumes.

And all the while, I could sense her, my mate, my Druid queen. She'd been scared, worried, and determined. But when it all came to an abrupt halt, when I couldn't feel anything but static air, the life damn near poured from my body. And when I caught sight of her falling to the ground unconscious, my heart seized for a solid two steady beats. All I could think about was how it couldn't happen—not a second time.

"Abby," I roared, sprinting away from the Dullahan and leaving the others to deal with him. They'd sure as hell understand, or if they had anything to say about it, they could fuck off. She needed me, and I made a promise. Never. Again.

"Please tell me it worked," Rhiannon whispered, clutching to Morrigan's side and glancing between a passed-out Abby and the Dullahan wailing behind me.

"Abby, grá, it's me." Sliding on my knees, I cradled her head and rested it on my lap, quickly swiping the blood from her nose away and wiping it on my pants.

Morrigan's painted crimson toes appeared in my line of vision. "She's fine, Druid. It was her first time using her Bandruí power at full strength. She was bound to exhaust herself."

Glowering at the Phantom Queen, I stroked Abby's head. "Then why did you not tell *her* that?"

"What have you done to me?" Crom bellowed behind us.

Morrigan's gaze flipped to the Dullahan before returning to me. "I couldn't have her holding back. It was the main reason we needed her to be immortal. It would've likely killed a mortal."

"I know we have a love-hate relationship, Mor, but—" I spoke through gritted teeth, unable to stop my limbs from shaking. "—I'm sure you can guess how I'm feelin' right about now."

Morrigan frowned and patted my head like a damned dog. I sneered and snapped my head away from her touch. "You should know I never do anything if I'm not confident of the outcomes. Abby's bloodline is extremely powerful, and her bond with you will render her unstoppable one day if she harnesses this power."

Abby's tattoo made several faint red glitches, and she whimpered.

"Bloodline? You know about her family?" The anger hadn't dissipated; in fact, it boiled at the surface now, waiting to explode. "Did you plan to tell her about any of it?"

"If she wishes to know, Erimon, she'll *ask*." Morrigan snapped her robes behind her and strolled past me, latching onto Rhiannon's hand and leading her away.

Shaking my head because I planned to deal with *that* particular problem later, I traced my thumb over Abby's cheeks as her eyes fluttered open. "Abby, it's me. You're alright."

Gasping, Abby sat up straight, her hand immediately flying to the spot on her chest where the Dullahan had previously impaled her with his whip.

As urgently as that last time, I slapped my palm over it. "That didn't happen this time, grá. You're fine. Got a bit overwhelmed with your powers, is all."

Abby grimaced and grasped one of my shoulders for purchase as if it were the only thing capable of grounding her. "We were saying the chant and this blinding flash, and Crom was roaring and—"

What started as panic overtaking her expression shifted to hatred in one breath. She gazed behind me, glaring at who I could imagine was the being of the hour—the Dullahan. Abby's tattoo blazed a fierce red, and she pushed to her feet, only allowing me to help her ensure she wouldn't fall.

If this doesn't work, I'll have Morrigan's head.

Her voice, full of determination and fury, still managed to maintain that buttery undertone.

Raking a hand through my hair, I sighed and turned, watching Abby storm toward the group standing around a vulnerable Crom.

And I wouldn't stop ye, but she's not easy to get rid of.

"Out of the way," Abby ordered, shouldering past Finn and Cu, who gladly stepped aside.

They arched their brows at me, and I dusted my palms at the prospect of stopping her. Not after all she'd been through to get here. She deserved every satisfactory moment and she was about to receive a goldmine.

"Is this the same *person*?" Abby asked Morrigan, pointing at a male on his knees, his head held low, long chestnut locks falling in unruly shambles over his face.

"Yes. This is Crom before he came to be the Dullahan. It's how he started and how he shall live out the rest of his days. Unable to invoke chaos every century now." Morrigan tilted her head at Crom. "Isn't that right, Crom?"

Crom didn't look at us initially, his fists pressing into the stone floor. "You have no idea what you've done giving Balor full reign."

"Morrigan," Abby said, her tone resembling someone about to get the news she didn't want to hear.

Morrigan patted Abby's shoulder and gave a quick smile. "Do you honestly think I didn't see Balor's future desires for more power? He's your classic tale of narcissistic second-chance villains. It won't be a decade from now or even a century, but yes, he will try to continue the Dullahan chaos at some point in time."

Edging closer but not interfering, I pressed a finger between Abby's shoulder blades to let her know I was there for her.

She didn't look at me but reached behind her, grabbed my hand, and yanked me into the group. This smallest, seemingly trivial gesture brought a warm smile to my lips.

Crom finally lifted his chin, revealing his true face. Much to my chagrin, it wasn't the haggardly, withering type of the Crom I'd met. This Crom had thick brows, a strong jaw, deeply brown eyes, and a roguish, handsome charm about him that I'd never admit out loud to anyone.

You're way hotter than a former headless horseman who impaled me with a spine whip, grá.

Abby squeezed my hand, and I squeezed back.

"Knowing this, why would you give him that power?" Crom's Irish accent in this form sounded ancient and thick, much like my own when I'm in the right company, and it wouldn't raise suspicion. Crom squinted. then glared.

"Because now—" Morrigan curled an arm around Abby's shoulders. "—we have her. And if you hadn't played your part, we wouldn't. I'd be a little more thankful, Crom."

Crom's head began to shake, and he stood slowly, eliciting everyone's battle stances. "Curse you, witches."

Rhiannon lifted a finger and leaned in, "I'm not precisely a witch but more of a—"

Delicately, Finn slid a massive hand over Rhiannon's mouth, engulfing most of her face, and slowly coaxed her back.

"You are the cursed one here, Crom. No longer will you have access to the Otherworld unless you die; the Ninth Wave will never permit you. You'll spend the rest of your days on Earth, walking amongst mortals. What you do with that time is entirely up to you." Morrigan lifted an arm, the glowing runes appearing and vibrantly flashing. "And this—" She flicked one hand at the head still resting on the ground behind us. "You can go *fetch*."

The head disappeared in a swirl of fog and orange dust, going to where the gods only knew, hidden away from Crom's reach.

Crom stepped forward with an outstretched hand, his eyes blazing with utter fury. "I will spend every waking moment plotting a way to ruin you, Morrigan. And you—" Crom glared at Abby, and my tattoo raged with heat just from that one expression. "—don't think this is over."

"But it is, Crom," Abby replied, calm and collected. She neared him, and my body tensed. The compulsion to step between them, to protect her, was overwhelming, but I stood my ground. "And I hope you take this *blessing* we've given you and find a different path. Don't be like Balor. You're different."

"How the dubnos would you know, Bandruí?" Crom smirked and produced the golden shackles from inside his shirt sleeve. "And don't think for a second any of you are getting these back."

Patrick hissed under his breath.

Abby swirled her hands, palm over palm, producing what looked like a fireball but soon blossomed into something else entirely—a magical mass of stardust and power. "And because I know you can't find it in you to say to me, so I'll say it to *you*, Crom." Abby sucked in a deep breath. "Thank you. Were it not for you, I wouldn't have found my true calling, this family, or my mate."

Elders, was there nothing this woman couldn't do?

Crom's lip curled back, and he sneered, not responding to Abby.

"Have fun on the surface, Crom. It's not all that bad if you make the most of it." Abby hurled the magic orb at Crom, and despite his continued wailing protests and widened eyes, he disappeared until only the shackles remained, clanking to the ground.

Patrick frantically scooped them into his palms like someone else would've attempted to steal them. He went so far as to clutch them like a precious heirloom.

"You weren't exaggerating. You *do* learn quickly," Morrigan said, folding her arms and gazing at Abby in a new light.

Abby rubbed her thumb and forefinger together, a deep thought making her forehead cinch. "There's still so much you need to teach me."

"Just say when Abby. We can start as soon as you like."

Finn cleared his throat and moved to the center of the space, garnering everyone's attention. "I, for one, think we deserve a bit of R&R after that ordeal. Say, Mave, do your descendants still put that castle up for rent like they used to? The one in Galway?"

"Yes," Mave said hesitantly.

Finn was nothing more than a colossal teddy bear when he wasn't on the battlefield.

"Finn, are you seriously suggesting we rent a vacation castle?" Patrick asked, his eyes twinkling at the prospect.

"The man's gone daft," Cu mumbled.

"I don't know, Erimon, what would you say to it?" Finn moved his hands to his hips, drumming his fingers there.

"There is the small matter of our coronation first?" I arched a brow at Finn.

Mave waved me off. "That'll take an hour at most. Think of it as a bleedin' honeymoon if you have to."

"A honeymoon? With us all in earshot?" Cu grumbled.

Beaming at Abby, I turned her to face me and trailed my knuckles down her soft cheek. "What do you say, gra? It's big enough to still give us privacy." I'd elongated the "i" in the word and bobbed my brows.

"I think I'd be a fool to turn it down. And Phoebe will be ecstatic," Abby replied, curling her arms around my neck and kissing me.

"To Galway," Finn shouted, raising a fist in the air.

"Can I bring Estrella?" Rhiannon asked.

I held my Bandruí in my arms, fascinated by her power and fortitude. Yet, parts of her human upbringing still shone through. Grazing my nose with hers, I pulled her tighter and sighed into her hair. For the first time since we met in that pub, we could finally just be Erimon and Abby. Druid High King and Queen.

23

ABBY

IT WAS OVER. I COULD hardly believe it. After all this time, after all the danger, blood, sweat, and tears, we'd *defeated* the Dullahan. There was no telling the other risks we would face, but my burden, for however long the universe saw fit, was lifted. Briefly reuniting with Phoebe to deliver the news had brought me to tears. She's been a part of this ordeal from the beginning, even roped herself into this mythical world to help save my life. The only comfort I had when having to pull away from her embrace so quickly to go play royalty was knowing a castle retreat awaited.

Erimon and I stood before the Lia Fail stone, staring at it and stalling for time. We hadn't needed a telepathy bond to read each other's emotions—becoming majesties was as terrifying as it was exhilarating. It meant taking on extra responsibilities and upholding mythical duties bestowed on us, whatever those were. And me? I had so many questions. Would we be expected to attend ceremonies? Would I be expected to produce an heir?

Erimon chuckled and kissed my temple. "You worry too much, grá."

"They're valid and suitable concerns, Erimon." I knew he said it in an attempt to lighten my mood, but I wasn't having it.

He turned me to face him and lifted his palms only to rest them delicately on my shoulders. "Are you saying you don't wish to carry my devilishly handsome Druid spawn?"

"Erimon," I chastised, scrunching my nose and swatting his chest. "Definitely not when you call it *spawn*."

"I'm sorry, I'm sorry, but—" Erimon continued to snicker, his shoulders bouncing. "—you should see your face."

Tossing him an exasperated glare, I didn't respond this time.

"Right. Sorry." A frown pulled at his lips. "Whether one day you wish to bring a wee one into the world with me or you never speak a word of it, I'll be the happiest Druid to ever walk the land."

Sighing, I inched closer and rested my forehead on his collarbone. "And that means the world to me, but what if it's a duty the Elders expect?"

"Then I'd say, fuck 'em."

Leaning back, I widened my eyes at him. "The Elders?"

"Yeah." Erimon shrugged. "I'm going to be High King. That gives me commanding rights."

I narrowed my eyes. "Does it, though? Over The *Elders*?"

Erimon took my face in both hands and squished my cheeks together. "It'll all be right as rain, Abby. I *promise* ye."

Unlike before, when he'd made his promises, simply through words spoken or whispered, this time, it made my tattoo sizzle.

Erimon winced, glancing at his shimmering sapphire ink.

"What the dubnos was *that?*" Erimon trailed his touch over his arm, glaring at it like the tattoo planned to answer him itself.

Cinniúint.

Destiny. Fate. It may not have had a genuine voice, but it chose unique ways to speak to us.

"It would seem, my dear Druid—" I smoothed out his shirt before patting his sternum. "You really *are* tied to your promises with me now."

"*What?*" Erimon tilted his head to one side, closed his eyes, and shook his head. "Not that I don't plan to keep them, but when did that start?"

This was fun.

Shrugging, I latched onto his hand. "Maybe it's because of the whole marking deal you did to me."

Erimon rolled his eyes and gazed skyward. "Are you still goin' on about that? I thought you'd be flattered."

He was right. I was. The primal instinct of knowing I belonged to him spoke to an archaic side of me buried deep.

But I said nothing to him and touched the stone, taking us to the Hills of Tara, where the Elder's cottage awaited.

"I had that comin', didn't I?" Erimon said, yanking me to his side and nuzzling my neck, his beard tickling my chin.

"I surely hope something will be coming soon."

Erimon laughed, his minty breath wafting over my cheek. "That's supposed to be my line."

"Maybe *you* should be quicker." I flashed him a sparkling grin because I was so far gone for this male.

"And maybe you two should get your arses in here," the

Elder said from the open doorway.

We jolted to attention, our bodies going stiff. While staring at the Elder, I fished for Erimon's hand and clung to it before we walked inside.

The Elder moved to a stone pillar in the room's center, where two crowns rested on an emerald green satin pillow. The larger one consisted of golden overlapping twigs curved into a circular shape with the ends sprouting at the back. Leaves speckled with tiny emeralds were interwoven into the design. The smaller one, a circlet tiara, was similar. But it bore tiny golden acorns, varying types of flowers encrusted with diamonds and amethyst, and hanging at the point was a Celtic infinity symbol ending in a diamond teardrop.

"Elder, wait," Erimon blurted, holding up his palms.

The Elder and I gave him the same befuddled stare.

"Don't tell me you're backing out now, Erimon. Of all the—" The Elder beat his cane against the wooden floorboards.

"No, no, old man. Listen to me. I have but one question—" Erimon paused and rubbed his fingers together. "—or two, or three, before we settle this."

The Elder puckered his lips and nodded. "That's fair." He rested his withered hands atop the cane. "Ask."

"What are our main duties? Times have changed since the first High King. We're not exactly at war with orcs, trolls, or otherwise any longer." Erimon twirled his rings.

"Any affairs that arise within the Celtic ethereal community involving the gods, creatures, or heroes, if they call for council, you'll serve as such."

Erimon played with his rings more chaotically now. "Right.

Makes sense. And uh, ceremonies, balls, celebrations, and the like. Would we be expected to attend them?"

He was asking the questions *I* wanted to ask. If I could only fall for this man all over again.

"Of course. If you're invited. Not many hold them in this day and age, though, I'm afraid. A lost art, if you ask me." The Elder scratched the side of his nose.

Erimon slowly nodded and closed his hand into a fist to keep from fidgeting. "And finally—"

Grabbing his bicep, I gulped and shook my head. "Monny, you don't have to ask that."

"He's right here, gra. If it'd put you at ease, now's the time to ask." Erimon squeezed my hand.

Licking my lips, feeling my heart pounding erratically in my chest, I lifted my chin and came out with it. "Will it be considered a duty of *mine* to produce an heir?"

The Elder's bushy brows rose, and he appeared sincerely taken aback. "That's entirely up to you and fate, my dear child."

A relief washed over me. There was no saying I'd never want to have our own Druid family, but knowing now that the decision lay entirely on me and Erimon, it meant the universe and stars to me.

"Thank you for clarifying, Elder." I offered him a warm smile.

The Elder drummed his fingers on his cane. "Anything else?"

Abby?

I brushed our tattoos together, humming at the velvety, soothing sensation it gave.

I'm good. No. I'm great.

"I think we're all set. Let's do this thing," Erimon answered, winking at the Elder.

The Elder shook his head. "You always were so eloquent with your words. If you'd both approach the pillar, please."

With our hands still entwined, we stood in front of the Druid Elder, ready to accept another destiny. The Elder held his staff with both hands, a bright light surging through it, revealing Celtic markings carved into it down its length.

"Kneel," the Elder beseeched.

Together, we knelt before him, never letting go of one another, our ink markings blazing so fiercely on our arms it was almost blinding.

The Elder raised the staff above Erimon's head first. "Do you, Erimon, accept the role and duty of High King?"

"I do."

When the staff moved to me, faeries seemed to flutter their wings over my skin. "Do you, Abigail, accept the role and duty of High Queen to rule alongside your King?"

Smiling, resplendently, and deliriously happy, I responded, "I do."

The Elder slammed the staff to the ground, and it stood upright. He took the larger crown in his grasp and slid it over Erimon's head, followed by the smaller one on mine. When we glanced at each other, we both grinned. The firelight from overhanging sconces danced in the golden twigs' reflection on Erimon's crown and made the gems twinkle.

"And so it is done this day," the Elder concluded, simply sitting on a stool by the fire and coughing.

Erimon did a double take. "That's it?"

"Yes, that's it. What'd you expect? A parade of chariots,

trumpets, and rolled-out green carpet?" The Elder smirked, coughing again into his fist.

"Not exactly, but if that's all it took, why didn't you do this before we fought the Dullahan? Saved us another trip?" Erimon asked.

"Oh? Don't want an excuse to visit your Elder?"

Erimon sighed, his shoulders slumping forward. "That's not what I meant."

"I had to make sure you both would make it out alive. To be named king and queen only to have you both wind up dead would've been awkward and unfortunate." The Elder scratched the back of his head.

A laugh wanted to push from my throat at the absurdity of it all. "You had that much faith in us, did you?"

"Faith had nothing to do with it. I have to uphold my duty, just as you do. And that meant initiating *living* beings."

A faint beeping sound went off from Erimon's trousers. He frowned and snatched the pager, eyes scrolling the small screen. "Patrick's calling a meeting of Team Druid."

"A meeting? Do you think it's Crom?"

Erimon's expression turned grave. "I don't know, but he gave latitude and longitude markings. I can port us there as soon as—"

We turned our attention to the Elder, who was already waving us off. "Go, go. You two still have a lot of destinies to answer to."

"Thanks again, old man. I promise I won't be a stranger," Erimon said, wincing as soon as he said it, closing his eyes and opening one when his tattoo didn't react the same way it had with me.

"Yeah, yeah. Go on." The Elder smiled and encouraged us on our way.

Grinning as we walked to the stone, I swayed our joined hands. "Yup. You're mine, High King Erimon. Promises and all."

"Come here, High Queen." Erimon pressed a hand to my back and pulled me against him, merging his mouth with mine in a planet-altering kiss that left my knees weak.

When he finally pulled away, he lured me in with his captivating sky eyes and said, "And that is how I confirm that you, too, are *so* mine."

Together, we touched the stone, which returned us to modern Ireland, and Erimon whisked us away to where the group called for us.

24

ERIMON

CALL ME PARANOID, GIVEN THE past year's events, but when Patrick used the pager to summon me anywhere, I got overwhelmingly concerned for Abby's wellbeing. Should I have recognized the markers he gave did not lead to his hovel? Probably. But the urge to protect and provide for my mate had become so imperative lately that I hadn't given it a second thought. To my sheer delight, however, we stood in front of a massive castle in Galway instead.

"They've already rented the castle?" Abby whistled while gawking at the massive piece of architecture standing before us. "They work fast."

"Almost too fast," I grumbled, still on edge and not yet near convinced this wasn't some kind of a setup.

Abby hooked her arm with mine and pulled me toward the entrance. "Let's go knock."

"Oh, how you've changed, gra," I said, chuckling and letting her lead me to the door.

Abby paused and tossed me a bewildered expression. "How so?"

"When we first met, you were extremely cautious, guarded, and what did you call it?" I snapped my fingers. "A worrywart. And now you're waltzing up to a strange door with no clue at what lies on the other side without a care in the world."

Abby blinked several times, her gaze falling to the gravel driveway before lifting. "You're right. It seems I've become more unburdened than I realized."

"Don't mistake it for something bad." Kissing her head, I coaxed her onto the stone stoop. "Just promise me you won't lose *all* your caution." I give her a playful smirk, making the corners of my eyes glint the way I knew she liked.

"Or—" Abby, without warning, knocked on the door. "—I could give you a taste of your old medicine for a change."

My shoulders tense, my hand ready to pull apart the door to create a sword if the situation called for it. "The Elder wasn't enough? You have to be in on it, too?"

Abby laughed and rested her head on my arm while we waited for the door to open—if anyone answered.

Slowly and suddenly, the door creaked open, revealing nothing but perpetual darkness within. Abby lifted her head, sobering her tone. She snatched the seax I'd given her from its hilt, holding it behind her back, and I conjured iron to my palm, molding it and ready to hurl it at whatever stood on the other side. We side-stepped in time with each other, walking into a quiet, abandoned atrium with twin spiraling marble staircases.

Where in the dubnos is everyone?

I'd spoken it telepathically to Abby rather than whisper it out loud because we *could*.

And who opened the door?

Abby thought back.

Dozens of lights, including the massive crystal and gold chandelier above us, illuminated to life, and seven heads popped up from varying hiding places. Abby raised the dagger in a striking gesture while I curled my arm behind me with the awaiting iron.

"Surprise," the heads shouted in unison.

Finn moved from behind a burgundy velvet curtain hanging over a floor-to-ceiling window with his hands up defensively. "Hold yer horses now, Monny. It's just us."

They were all here—Finn, Cu, Mave, Patrick, Phoebe, Rhiannon and her *unicorn*.

Abby blew out a relieved breath. "That certainly got my heart racing."

"What are you all doing here so early?" I asked, grinning and squelching my power from my palm.

"Look, they're still wearing their crowns. How quaint," Finn announced.

Cu pointed at us and elbowed Mave in the ribs. "Those are a lot fancier than yours, I noticed."

"As they should be." Mave batted his hand away as Cu continued to prod her. "They're Druidic royalty. I was lucky they even had enough iron to make mine."

"We wanted to throw you a surprise coronation party, so Mave pulled a few strings and booked the castle early." Phoebe jumped excitedly and pressed her hands together.

Abby's raven flew over them, his shiny, onyx wings flapping with strong strokes until he found her contentedly perching on her shoulder. He nuzzled his head against her chin, and Abby visibly relaxed from the avian contact.

Sheepishly, her cheeks turning rosy, Abby reached for her crown like she was about to take it off. "I forgot I was wearing it."

"Hey," I whispered, delicately halting and coaxing her hand away. "Don't be ashamed of it. And if they wish to throw us a coronation party, I damn well think we should be wearing them, don't you agree?"

She nodded, and I slipped an arm around her waist.

And perhaps tonight that'll be the only *thing you're wearin'.*

Grinning at me, Abby arched a wicked brow.

"Should a party not have a form of music?" Rhiannon asked, leaning on her unicorn and stroking its body.

My ethereal friends shared silent glances before Phoebe saved the day with a resounding, "Already on it. I brought a dock for my phone to stream through a speaker."

"I see they've made a few upgrades to the castle through the years. Electricity? Wireless internet?" Finn mentioned, barking in laughter.

"No kidding. Even indoor plumbing," Mave added, and they both chuckled.

Cu disappeared several moments before returning with wooden crates on his shoulders. "And I brought what's most important." He set the containers on a nearby table, the contents clanking together. "Booze."

A song with Irish pipes and fiddles played through the vast space, echoing off the walls. Phoebe trotted back to Patrick, all smiles and bouncing auburn hair.

Finn grabbed a bottle from Cu's stash, popped the cork, and drank straight from the source. "So, Abby—" He wiped his sleeve over his mouth and beard. "—how's it feel to not only have the Dullahan off your back but now you're an immortal Bandruí *queen?*"

With drinks in hand, everyone turned to Abby expectantly, waiting for her to answer.

"Oof," Abby started, running her knuckle over the bird's crest. "Honestly, I've barely had a chance to let it all sink in until now."

"Precisely." Mave shoved Finn and Cu aside as she moved to Abby and held a small bottle out to her. "Let her Majesty have a few drinks and relax before you go and ask something so serious."

Her majesty.

Bleedin' Elders. I was High King. We were overseers of the fantastical Celtic varieties. If someone would have told me a thousand years ago that I would become this, that I'd be mated to a mortal turned Bandruí female, and that not only would Finn, Mave, and Cu become some of my best friends but a damned Leprechaun too? Shite. I'd have laughed in their face and cursed their very name. But that's why it took this long to bring us all together. A thousand years ago, Abby had yet to be born. A thousand years ago, the rest of them, much like myself, were very different beings. This, right here, was the utmost perfect moment.

Hours went by as we partied into the night, dancing, telling jokes, and reliving past memories that, in hindsight, weren't that long ago but seemed decades ago. I'd shared countless wayward glances at Abby, marveling at her resplendent beauty and how the crown suited her more than I could've ever anticipated. Cu had brought the "good stuff," a type of alcohol that allowed immortals to get an actual buzz. But here I was, pounding them back like it was mortal whiskey, and I felt rather blissful and deliriously happy.

"All, I wanted to bring this up before, but I wasn't sure how to say it," Rhiannon started, burping and draping a hand over her unicorn's back, the only solid thing keeping her standing at this point in the evening.

"This oughta be good," Mave answered, snorting and hiccupping.

Abby was seated on my lap, the raven happily munching on a piece of bread she'd given him on the floor at our feet. I quickly pecked her cheek because I truly couldn't help myself.

Rhiannon took another swig before raising the glass above her head. "Cu is always naked after his spasm-abob, and no one bats an eyelash?"

The rest of us exchanged glances because I'd imagine they were thinking the same thing I was, that I'd completely forgotten about his nudity, and the last thing I wanted to gawk at was his hound cock.

"My dear," Mave started, moving to Rhiannon's side and curling her arm about her shoulders. "We've been around the big brute long enough to know that if you've seen one giant dick swinging around, you've seen them all. We pay it no mind and go about our day."

"Giant?" Cu asked, a confident smile edging his lips.

Mave pointed at him and narrowed her eyes. "Do not make more out of that than it is, *hound*."

Cu bucked his hips, making the center of the leather belt bounce. Mave's gaze snapped straight to it, and Cu and Finn called her out on it, breaking into a maniacal bout of chuckling.

Abby combed my beard with her fingers, still sporting the same grin that hadn't left all night.

"What you thinkin'?" I asked, bumping my knuckle under her chin.

"You can't *hear* me?"

Snickering, I adjusted her crown, which had tilted to one side. "Not when you're not thinking nothin'."

"I guess I was wondering, since everyone else is here, where is—"

A swirl of grey smoke and black feathers appeared at the room's center, Morrigan presenting herself with a snap of her robes.

"—Morrigan," Abby finished.

Recollections of the bullshit that Morrigan pulled with the Dullahan still lay fresh in my mind, but it was a matter to be dealt with when we were not celebrating.

"Why are you all looking at me like that?" Morrigan asked, dusting her sleeves and panning the room of angry glares.

"Did you not get the invitation?" Phoebe asked, pouting.

Morrigan sighed and clacked her black nails together. "Of course I did. I wanted to be here earlier, but other matters needed my attention first. Some of us have jobs to do *every* day, not just when something gets fucked."

Cu rolled his eyes and busied himself with his drink, further raising Mave's hackles by poking her ribs and tickling her.

"You're here now," Abby added with a weak smile.

"Yes, I am, your Majesty. And I'm here for you. Rather, to train you if you're ready." Morrigan moved closer to Abby, extending a hand for her to take. "I have somewhere I need to be that will take me the better part of a year, and I didn't want to leave you in a lurch that long."

"I don't know. I'm pretty intoxicated," Abby replied, wobbling on her stool.

Morrigan offered a genuine smile. How abnormal. "That's perfect. You won't always be in your best state when trouble arises. It'll be good practice." She motioned with her hand for Abby to stand.

"Watch Emrys for me, Mon, will you?" Abby stood and wiped her hands on her pants.

"Of course." I turned my gaze to Morrigan and pointed a stern finger. "No funny business, Mor."

"Not at all." Morrigan wrapped her arm around Abby and led her to a hallway. "There was also the matter of you learning to *mark* your Druid, wasn't there?"

Shite.

25

ABBY

WITH MY MIND IN A euphoric buzz, I followed Morrigan into an empty room with stone flooring. She removed her cloak, standing in a blood-red satin dress that matched the crimson sheen in her black hair when the firelight hit it at the right angle.

"Can you really do that? Show me how to mark him as mine, I mean?" I curled my hair around a finger like a shy teenager. The idea made my insides bubble, and the ink on my arm hum in anticipation.

"Oh, yes. It's a casting spell taught at the beginning stages for Druids and witches. And it will only work on your mate. That way, magical beings can't simply go around marking people as *theirs*." Morrigan scoffed and tossed some hair from her eyes.

"Let that be the last thing you show me. It'll be like a reward." I wickedly grinned at her.

Morrigan smiled back and tapped my nose with a finger. "I like you more and more, Bandruí."

Slapping my face several times in an attempt to be more attentive, I rolled my shoulders and propped my hands on my hips. "I'm all ears."

"Considering what I've seen you do thus far, harnessing more of your power will come down to continued practice. You'll also want one of these—" Morrigan reached into an invisible pocket in the air, producing a leatherbound book.

"Is that—" I gulped and stepped forward. "—a *spell* book?"

Morrigan peered at it like it were her child and trailed a delicate hand over it. "Yes. It was my first, and I wish for *you* to have it now."

I reached for it before she announced what the book meant to her and snatched my hand away like I'd catch it on fire. "Oh, Morrigan, I *couldn't*."

"Why not? I'm giving it to you. I know this book from cover to cover and have nothing else to learn from it. In fact—" She opened it and flipped through some of the pages, the drawings glowing radiant purple when her finger would brush one. "—I haven't had use for it in centuries, but for some reason—" Morrigan peered at me and slammed the book shut. "—I felt compelled to store it for safekeeping until the time was right."

Chewing on my thumbnail, I folded one arm over my stomach and paced a square. "It still doesn't feel right."

"Do you know who would've given you one of these if she could have?" Morrigan held the book on display with her palm between us.

I shrugged, mesmerized by the book now.

"Your *mother*."

Tears blurred my vision despite never knowing her. "Did

you *know* her?"

"I'm afraid not. But any witch with a daughter would pass down their spell book. And since yours was taken from you far too early, and I can never bear children, I want you to have it, Abby. Please." She held it out to me with both hands, a plea in her gaze that was so unlike her.

With shaking hands, I took the book and clutched it to my bosom like a security blanket. If only this would've been my mother's, at least I'd have some part of her to hold onto.

Morrigan tilted her head to one side. "Would you like to know more about your parents?"

"I thought you said you didn't know them personally?"

"I didn't." Morrigan rubbed the pentagram pendant hanging from a chain around her neck between two fingers. "But I have the power to let you see them through your eyes."

My eyes? Confusion rattled my brain, and I couldn't be sure if it was the alcohol or the overwhelming desire to know anything about my past, but it was enough to have me rocking back on my heels.

"How? I was a newborn when they died."

Nodding, Morrigan slipped a hand onto my shoulder. "Yes. But you still had eyes and a mind and spirit. It may be brief, but you'll be able to see what they looked like, possibly even hear their voices."

My bottom lip trembled, and I couldn't get the words out fast enough. "Yes. Yes, please. Show me."

Morrigan bowed her head. "Then close your eyes and settle your mind."

I'd have thought it more difficult to think about nothing on command, but my desire to know more about where I came from made it as easy as taking a breath.

My eyes lazily opened within seconds, but instead of seeing Morrigan, I saw a wooden ceiling. Gurgles and cooing floated from my throat, and a pair of the tiniest little hands lifted in front of me—*my* hands.

A female face appeared, leaning over me—she had my slanted nose, my full lips, and my same tanned skin tone. "I just can't get over how beautiful she is, Thalior."

Thalior. Who was Thalior?

"You'll meet her in due time, Emrys," a male voice said, followed by wings flapping and a familiar caw.

Emrys? My raven? It's—my *father's.*

My father stood beside her, peering down at me with a wistfully proud expression. His hand wrapped around the female's shoulders. He had my hazel eyes, snow-like pale skin, pointed ears, and long, deep, brown hair—exactly like *mine.* "We've certainly made a treasure, haven't we, Willa?"

Thalior and Willa. These were my parents. My birth parents had *loved* me.

I giggled and stretched my hands skyward, begging one of them to pick me up.

Willa, my mother, bent to tenderly kiss my head, some of her black hair fluttering against my eyelashes. "I hate that we have to leave so quickly. I've only gotten to hold her a handful of times." Her sapphire eyes filled with tears.

"I know, my love, I know." Thalior, my father, pulled Willa to him, hugging her and holding her as she began to sob. "But the seers are strengthening their numbers. And now that they've formed an alliance with the ogre hordes, we *need* to act fast."

The sound of my mother's sadness was enough to incite my own crying, which started as little whimpers before becoming blaring wails.

Thalior pulled away from Willa to rest a comforting hand on my chest, gently kneading there. "Shh, Eira. Shh. I'm sorry. I can only hope that one day you'll understand we had to do this to ensure your future, my sweetest daughter."

Eira. My name was Eira.

Sniffling, Willa slid her hands under me and lifted me, cradling me in her arms. "One last time, my little snowflake."

"Don't speak like that, love. We'll see her again," Thalior said, stroking Willa's wavy hair.

"I know," she whispered. "I just wanted to hold her." Willa bounced me and moved for a thatched window where the glass had frosted over.

Thalior wiped some frost away with his shirt sleeve, and though it was difficult for my fresh eyes to take it all in—there were numerous snow-capped mountains and a wide river in the distance, a waterfall over the cliff spilling into it. Snow fell from the grey skies in dust and clumps.

I was born in the winter.

"It's time, Willa," Thalior said, his thin lips forming a deep frown.

Willa nodded, not saying anything and clearly holding back tears as she handed me to another female. Her apron was itchy against my arm, and I instantly hated the feeling, my hands raising in the direction my mother walked away.

My tiny fingers spread as wide as they could go. Another burst of tears built in my throat until I couldn't see my parents any longer. I cried myself to sleep in the stranger's arms as she tried everything to comfort me.

My eyes flew open. Morrigan stood with both hands on my arms, keeping me upright. It was for good reason because all I wanted to do was sink into a clump on the floor from everything I'd just learned.

Despite my throat feeling scratchy with sand, I pushed out. "Were you able to see all of that? Hear it?"

Morrigan nodded, concern evident in her gentle expression.

"Do you know what war they were talking about? Where *was* that?" I shrugged away from her touch, hanging my head in my hand and rubbing my temple.

"You were born in another realm. I've never been there, so I couldn't tell you which one."

I pressed a hand against my mouth, replaying the images of my mother and father until they were permanently etched on my brain. "So, I wasn't born on earth, but—" Pausing, I recalled the Elder's words and tears blurred my vision. "—by faeries and starlight."

"I wish I could tell you more." Morrigan slid her sleeves back to her wrists.

Turning, I cupped Morrigan's elbow and waited until she looked at me. "Thank you for doing that. Truly."

"It was my pleasure, *Eira*." Morrigan grinned.

I rested a hand on the back of my neck. "My birth-given name. It makes Abby seem meaningless now, yet it's the only name I've ever known."

"Perhaps you could go by both? In time, Eira may become the only name everyone *else* knows."

Smiling at this prospect, I retrieved the spell book. "Maybe."

"Now then. Flip to a random page, and barring it isn't one that'll turn Finn into a toad, we'll practice casting it until you get it right. And we'll keep flipping pages through the night until you have a good grasp on it. Deal?" Morrigan extended her hand.

I went to shake it but paused. "What if it's a spell that turns *Cu* into a toad?"

Morrigan cackled and smacked my hand away, motioning to the table. "You and I are destined to be great friends. And I needn't have the gift of sight to see that. And don't think I've forgotten about the marking spell. That'll be the icing on the cake."

Offering her a warm smile, I opened the book to a random page and pointed. "This one."

Morrigan turned it to face her, and she tapped the withered page with her pointy fingernail. "A productivity spell. Good one to start with. Now—"

We spent the entire night practicing proper hand movements, where to use the correct accents and emphasis on words within the spells, and we covered dozens of them. Each page made me feel more connected to my mother, Willa. Now that I had a face and voice to imagine as I became more familiar with my power, it pulled a strength from me that had yet to breach the surface. In my heart and soul, I knew she would be *proud* now if she were here.

26

ERIMON

EVER SINCE MORRIGAN WHISKED ABBY away to shower her with witchcraft, I effectively stopped drinking. I was too consumed with wondering what they were doing in there, especially how close it was to bleedin' sunrise. It'd gotten so bad that I stared at the wall as if I could see through several rooms and pinpoint the one they were in. After a growing headache and a bulging vein in my temple, I concluded that magical sight wasn't in my ethereal repertoire.

Finn jolted me from my daydreaming when he flopped onto the bench next to me and drunkenly slapped an arm across my back. "So, what's it like having a fated mate, old friend?"

His question gave me genuine pause, and I rubbed my new bonding ring on my left hand, the sight of it pulling a smile from my lips. "To be honest, Finn, not how I thought it would make me feel."

Finn paused mid-drink and looked around us like I was about to reveal something scandalous. "Oh, boy. I don't like the sounds of that."

"No, no." Chuckling, I clapped him on the shoulder. "It's the opposite of being tied down like I thought it would be in my youth. It's *freeing*."

"Yeah?" Finn sighed and leaned his forearms on his thighs. "How'd you know it was her?" When he asked, he didn't look at me and flicked his thumb against his mug.

"That's hard to answer." I rubbed my chin. "I guess it started as a physical sensation. A sort of tingling down my spine I'd never felt before when I first saw her. Gradually, it came together mentally and emotionally until it felt like the universe seized me by the balls and told me she was it."

Finn nodded, tapping his fingertips against the mug now, his gaze lifting across the room where Rhiannon laughed and chatted with Mave. "I'd be lyin' if I said I wasn't a bit envious."

I bumped my shoulder against Finn's. "You don't need a fated mate to be happy, MacCoul. In fact, if you waited for it, you might end up like I did."

"A stubborn, selfish, jaded arsehat?" Finn eyed me sidelong and arched a thick blonde brow.

"You could've at least let me call myself those things." Smirking, I took a sip of my stout, grimacing at how warm it'd gotten. "I'm serious. You should talk to her, and now—" I knocked on Finn's mug. "—is the *perfect* time."

Finn sat straighter. "Dammit, you're right." He stood, finished his drink, tossed his mug absently behind him, which I caught, and strode toward Rhiannon.

Now, I could add "matchmaker" to my growing list of titles.

I need you.

Abby's sweet voice trickled over my brain, making me shudder, and my cock instantly hardened. My wings fanned out, tearing through my shirt like they were suddenly directly connected to my dick.

"For fuck's sake," Cu grumbled from somewhere nearby.

Ignoring him, I threw the mugs on a nearby table and stormed for the hallway, my nose perked to detect her scent. After passing five doors, I sensed her presence behind the sixth, and my tattoo shimmering to life convinced me its other half was behind this door.

Testing the knob, I grinned when it freely turned and stepped inside. My heart skipped several beats at the sight of a naked Abby sprawled on a bed of white and emerald satin sheets. Her bronze skin positively glowed as she parted her hair from her chest, revealing those luscious breasts I wanted in my mouth as soon as inhumanly possible.

Abby propped herself on her elbows, a sultry wickedness playing in her gaze before she splayed her hand and turned my clothes to *ash*. After ogling my steadily flapping wings, her eyes dropped straight to my very ready cock, and she nibbled her lip.

Flexing my arms, I strode across the room, flashing her my "sexy squint" once I reached the foot of the bed. Only a few hours apart, and something was different about her. I couldn't be sure whether it was her settling into her Bandruí power or something else entirely, but it was a question that could wait.

Crawling across the bed, I groaned when she slowly spread her legs for me, and I nestled between them, rubbing myself against her wetness. Abby moaned and tilted her head back, her fingers wrapping in my hair and pulling me to her chest.

I swirled my tongue over one nipple before taking it fully into my mouth.

"You know," I whispered, my voice huskier than usual. Positioning myself at her entrance, I gradually began to push into her. "This is the first time we're doing this, *not* in the forest."

Grinning, Abby wrapped her legs around me and pulled me the rest of the way into her, making me grunt when her warmth tightened around my length. "And let's not make a habit of it. It's far too normal for us."

Chuckling, I rocked in and out of her, resting one forearm on the bed beside her and using my other hand to trace my thumb over her forehead, down her nose, and lips. I cupped her cheek and stared down at her with an expression meant only for her—one of appreciation and absolute devotion.

Suddenly, Abby slid an arm around me and hoisted herself up, pushing my back to the bed and straddling my hips. Grimacing at first from the wings being squished, I sheathed them and stared at my mate heatedly.

What are you up to?

She pressed a finger to her lips, mischief waltzing in her caramel eyes. "Shh." As she gyrated her hips, she scraped her nails down my chest and stomach, whispering something I couldn't decipher. Our tattoos shimmered, glittered, and blazed so brightly it lit up the entire room. Abby's mouth pressed against mine, her tongue deviously licking my bottom lip before inviting itself in, intertwining with my own. A tingle pulse at the base of my spine. and I stiffened before blasting my eyes open, peering at a very satisfied Druidess. Her honeyed scent had become overwhelming. and if I stared long enough, a hazy hue would seem to border her frame now.

A deep chuckle pushed from my throat. "You wicked little witch. You've marked me, haven't ye?"

"I told you, Druid," she purred as she leaned over me, her breasts pressing to my chest. "I learn quickly." Abby's nose brushed my neck, taking a long inhale, breathing me in. "That's not a problem, is it?" Her tone was amused and delighted because she knew I didn't give a fuck.

Sitting up, I curled my hand around the back of her neck and kissed her. "Not at all. I hope they can smell your mark on me from kilometers away, *luachmhar.*"

Abby's smile at that was one they could write hymns about, and she wrapped her arms around my shoulders, still breathing our marked scents into her lungs.

After we'd made love, I lay with her curled against me, making languid strokes down her curves with my fingers. She'd been quiet longer than usual, but I shared the silence and waited.

She turned to face me suddenly, her arms curled against her chest, pushing her breasts together. "I saw my parents, Erimon."

"What?" I heard what she said but couldn't make sense of it.

"Morrigan. She let me see them through my eyes when I was a baby. It was the last time they saw me before—" Abby trailed off and closed her eyes.

Before they died.

Kissing her forehead, I rubbed up and down her arm, waiting for her to continue if she so wished.

"I'm from another realm. They were going off to fight in some war. I was born in the winter. Their names were Willa and Thalior." Abby rattled off everything like she was bound to forget it if she weren't quick enough and then paused, her bottom lip trembling.

"What is it, Abby?"

She winced at her name. "My real name is *Eira*."

Our tattoos blazed so brightly that they became blinding. The heat surging from mine was enough to actually hurt this time. I pressed my inked arm against hers, and the sensation dulled, followed by the light intensity until they were their normal glow.

"Eira," I repeated. "That's beautiful."

Abby pressed her folded hands against her lips. "Is it?"

"Very. Do you want to be called this now?"

It was perplexing to call her anything different from Abby or Abigail, considering that's how we'd met. But if it tied her to her genuine chimerical past, who was I to be selfish if she wished to latch onto it?

She shrugged. "I don't know. That name ties me to my parents, but I met you as Abby. I met Phoebe as Abby. It still means so much to me."

"Well—" Curling one arm around her, I rested my chin on her head. "—why don't I call you both? Surprise you with which one I'll say until you decide?"

Abby peeled back. "You'd do that?"

I pinched her chin, holding her face steady on mine. "I'd do *anything* for you, grá."

"I'd appreciate that."

"It's settled then. But I do have to advocate that I love the sound of Eira and Erimon." Smiling, I displayed my hand above us, picturing it.

"They do sound good together."

A vase crashed against a nearby room's wall, making us tense.

"What the hell was that?" Abby asked, sitting up and fumbling for her clothes.

"I don't know, but we should check it out." Wrapping the sheet around my waist, we clamored into the hallway, staring at the numerous doors.

"I hate you so bleedin' much," a male's voice roared from one room.

"Was that *Cu?*" Abby asked.

We paused only a moment longer before finding the correct door.

"Then show me, you bastard," Mave yelled.

Sighing, I gazed skyward. "Fuck. It was only a matter of time before those two had a go at each other."

"We should stop them," Abby whispered, jutting her chin at the doorknob.

Nodding, I whisked open the door—and immediately regretted it.

Mave was butt naked, bent over a roll desk with the hulking form of Cu ferociously thrusting behind her.

All four of us paused, frozen stiff, as we tried to gauge how to react to this new development. Abby elbowed me in the side, bringing me back to the present.

Holding the sheet tighter around my hips with one hand, I waved at Mave and Cu with the other. "Carry on."

Mave raised a brow as if she was simply waiting for me to *leave.*

Backpedaling and tripping over the sheet, we returned to

the hallway, and I slammed the door behind us.

"Don't think that's going to make me stop," Cu said from within the room.

"I'd *kill* you if you did," Mave replied.

I cleared my throat. "Well, that was fun. Care to get some sleep? If we *can* now?"

Abby laughed and hugged my side. We walked back to our designated bedroom, curled under the sheets, and fell contentedly asleep.

That afternoon, we emerged from our cocoon to the alluring smells of coffee, biscuits, sausage, and eggs wafting from the dining hall. Phoebe and Patrick had been busy in the kitchen preparing a brunch for everyone. When we arrived, Phoebe was placing the table and bouncing on her heels when she spotted us.

"Good morning, sleepy heads," Phoebe said, hugging me and then Abby. "I hope you're hungry."

Finn sat next to Rhiannon at the table, chatting and smiling, her damned unicorn standing in a corner eating something out of a metal bowl. Cu and Mave arrived shortly after us, taking seats on opposite sides of the table as if they hadn't fucked each other hours prior. Typical of them. Patrick waltzed in with a silver tray, resting it at the table's center with multiple silver carafes and ceramic cups with saucers.

Finn sniffed the air, one nostril twitching. His gaze panned the room, and he lifted his chin to take another whiff at the surrounding air.

Not making eye contact with him, I pulled the chair out for Abby and motioned for her to sit, pushing her in once she did.

Finn leaned toward me, sniffing me, and barked with laughter, slapping the table and making plates and utensils bounce. "And now you *both* reek of Druid. Bleedin' hilarious."

Abby's cheeks turned rosy, and she squeezed my knee beneath the table.

"Eat up," Patrick said, grinning and sitting beside Phoebe.

Abby's raven flew from its perch, resting on the table near Abby and waiting for biscuit crumbles she'd hand-feed him. Team Druid sat at the table, enjoying a meal together without the burden of a looming Dullahan or fearing for Abby's life. It. Was. Grand.

Phoebe sighed. "I wish we could all just live here."

Forks clanked against plates, jaws dropped, and all eyes widened at Phoebe.

Patrick's lip twitched, and he pulled his phone from his pants pocket. "As you wish, my dear."

"Oh my—" Phoebe gasped and slapped a hand over her mouth. "—but I didn't. Crap."

The leprechaun promise to their eternal brides: three wishes for every year.

Abby smiled and hid it with her hand.

After dialing a number, Patrick stood and pressed the phone to his ear. "Looks like I have some paperwork to file and a check to write, everyone. If you'd give me a moment." Patrick walked away, Phoebe sprinting after him.

Finn beat his finger on the table and glanced around. "Ye know, we *could* make this place our new headquarters. It sure beats Patrick's hovel."

"I like that idea," Abby beamed. "It could be a retreat or a refuge in between times for everyone."

Nodding, I let everyone sort it out for themselves, knowing I'd go with anything my mate wanted.

"If that's the case, we can't let Patrick cover the *entire* bill. It wouldn't be right." Mave reached into her skirts and plopped a satchel of coins on the table.

Finn freed the gold rings in his hair and beard, adding them to the pile. Rhiannon held her palm up and a pile of varying gemstones appeared from silver dust.

Abby shoved her hands between her knees, worry blatant on her face.

I yanked two rings from my fingers, the ones with the largest jewels, and tossed them in. "One of those is Abby's contribution."

Abby smiled at me and squeezed my thigh.

Mave kicked Cu underneath the table and widened her eyes at him.

"What?" Cu yelled, rubbing his shin.

"Don't act like you have nothing to spare, Hound. Give it up." Mave pointed at the treasure mountain forming on the table.

Cu rolled his eyes and snatched a knife from his hip. Its blade had gold filigree, and the solid gold hilt bore several jewels. He stabbed it into the table. "There. Happy?"

"Hardly," Mave answered with a sultry grin.

"Hey, now." Finn pointed at the dagger sticking out from the table. "That's soon to be *our* table. You best start takin' care of it."

A knock sounded from the front door, putting us on the immediate defense.

Finn rose and motioned for the rest of us to stay put. "I'll see who it is."

Several moments later, we heard Finn say, "What the hell do *you* want?"

"I've come to collect," a familiar male voice answered.

The color drained from Mave's face. "Ilmarinen."

The bleedin' Finnish blacksmith who'd only made the enchanted golden shackles for us in exchange for Mave promising him her hand in fucking marriage. Was it too much to have hoped he'd forgotten the whole thing?

Growling, Cu stood, already starting the transformation into his warp-spasm form.

Mave held him back with a stiff arm. "Cu, don't. I have this handled."

Frowning, Cu sat and grunted.

Mave rose and slowly made her way to the atrium, adjusting her robes and flattening them with her palms. We followed behind her, prepared to give back up if necessary.

"Mave, my dear, there you are. I'm here to take you away from all of this. It is due time you uphold your end of the deal." Ilmarinen motioned for her to come to him.

Mave didn't move, standing several meters away and folding her arms. "Crom still lives. And as you can see—" She looked at Abby. "—so does she."

Ilmarinen looked nowhere else but at Mave. "Ah, but you see, Abigail *did* die."

"Can he do that?" Rhiannon asked, whispering it to Finn,

who'd joined her side.

Mave nodded. "I had a feeling you were going to say that."

"Then you know that you now belong to me. So let us go, shall we?" Ilmarinen referenced the open door.

Mave held her head low and moved closer to him. She pulled something from her robes that reflected the daylight from outside—a blade. She plunged it into Ilmarinen's neck, letting it stay there as he began to gurgle, a confused and shocked expression melting over his face.

"If you could speak, I'd imagine you're wondering how I knew your weakness was Ostilanide?" Mave grabbed Ilmarinen's face with one hand. "Hephaestus. Not only did he know what could kill you, but he also forged that dagger for me."

Finn leaned toward me and whispered, "When did she have time to do all that?"

"She's good like that," Cu answered for me, actually *smiling* at the sight of Mave.

"So, no, I will not be your betrothed, and you'll be where you belong." Mave shoved Ilmarinen, making him fall in a lifeless heap on the floor. "Dead."

Finn sighed and moved for the body. "Will someone help me with this? He's bleedin' all over *our* area rug."

Turning to Abby, to Eira, I took her hands in mine and rubbed my thumbs over her knuckles. "What do you say, my queen? Winters in an Irish castle and summers in a secluded woodland cottage?"

She brushed our tattoos, and the smile she gave me could revive a dying star. "I'll go wherever you are, Erimon. I'm eternally *yours*."

EPILOGUE

EIRA

Six months later…

SIGHING, I STROKED EMRYS' SOFT, feathered crest. "I wish I could talk to you. You must have so many stories about my parents. And don't think I haven't checked." I nudged my head toward the spell book Morrigan gave me resting on the table between us.

Emrys squawked, flapped his wings, and tilted his head from left to right. He waddled closer and delicately pressed his beak to my mouth—his best version of a kiss.

"Ra," Phoebe shouted from the doorway, sprinting inside with Patrick and Erimon trailing behind her.

Bracing for impact, I accepted her jubilant embrace and hugged her tight. "Phoebs," I crooned, still holding on. "It's been way too long."

"No kidding. Two months." Phoebe peeled back and gripped my shoulders. "But royal duties are of the utmost importance, so I understand. By the way, the cottage looks amazing. It looks so quaint from the outside, and then you come in here, and wow, it's *huge*."

Tugging on Phoebe's shirt sleeve, I tapped my finger on the book. "A cloaking spell. That way, people aren't as compelled to check it out *if* they happened to find it."

"You've always been so smart." Phoebe pinched my cheek before all but shoving me aside for my bird. "And there's my handsome man," her voice gained an octave and she offered her arm to Emrys, waiting for him to perch gleefully on it.

Flashing me with a bright grin, Erimon sidled beside me, curling an arm around my hips and kissing my cheek. "Hi ye, Snowy."

Snowy. I'd never get tired of that new nickname. We went months of him switching between Eira and Abby until one day, I asked to officially be Eira because it was the only genuine connection I had to my parents. Given that I was born in winter and they named me after the snow, Erimon soon started calling me Snowy, and I didn't dare stop him.

"How was town?" I asked, looking between him and Patrick.

Patrick carried several bushels of supplies, while Erimon only carried one. The two of them had started to get along far better than they had a year ago but still weren't a hundred percent. I doubted they ever would be.

"Bleedin' busy," Patrick answered, hoisting the bags on the table and wrapping his arms around Phoebe from behind her.

Erimon brushed his sleeve with mine, our tattoos beneath the fabric sparking to life. "An agonizin' twenty-three minutes for me without you there."

"Aw, you poor thing." I gave a quick peck to the tip of his nose.

Our times apart were always brief, but we still took them now and again to give each other a chance to breathe. Erimon had despised the idea at first given what he'd promised me, but I assured him that being only a few miles away for several minutes wouldn't break it by any means.

Phoebe rifled through the bags and shrieked when she pulled out a wheel of cheese. "Patty, you found it? As if I couldn't love you more."

Laughing, I elbowed Erimon's ribs. "That girl loves her cheese."

"I grabbed something for you too, grá." Erimon reached into his satchel and produced a bread loaf, handing it to me.

It was still warm, and I immediately tore a piece off—flaky, with just the right amount of crunch, and perfectly moist inside. Popping it into my mouth, I groaned—buttery, rich, and the slightest hints of sweet and cinnamon.

"Careful now. You're going to make me jealous of damned bread," Erimon teased, resting the bread on the counter.

"Thank you. It's the only market that *has* this bread." I dusted crumbs from my fingers and tried to peek at what else was in Erimon's bag.

To have a moment like this with Phoebe and Patrick in our woodland cottage provided a sense of peace. After our coronation celebration, we'd been thrown headfirst into all matters of duties—settling a land dispute, dealing with the Púca, and taming the man-wolves of Ossory. And those were more of the *major* grievances. Our crowns now rested on a white satin pillow near our bed until they were needed again. which I selfishly hoped was a bit longer.

"There's something else," Erimon started, his hand stuffed in the bag but not removing anything.

My throat tightened from the grave look on Erimon's face.

What is it?

I'd projected the question into Erimon's mind so as not to alert or worry Phoebe and Patrick.

Erimon pulled out a small scroll, resting the bag on the table and tossing it in his palm.

"Is that what I think it is?" I arched a brow, eyeing the rolled paper with a waxed seal I hadn't recognized.

"A summons," Erimon answered, catching my gaze with his.

Phoebe and Patrick appeared at our sides, and we stood in a circle, staring at the ominous, mysterious note resting between Erimon's fingers.

"What's it for?" Phoebe asked.

Erimon unfolded it and held it out to me. "It's from the King of the Greek gods."

"*Zeus?*" Patrick confirmed, surprise painted on his features.

Chewing on my thumbnail, I read the scroll to myself.

A summons for the Druidic High King and Queen

We request your presence in Greece as soon as possible to discuss matters of grievous importance. This matter could affect realms beyond the Greeks, and we are seeking any and all power willing to lend arms.

Zeus, King of the Greeks.

"Erimon, this sounds serious."

"I know, isn't it great?" Erimon grinned but let it fall away when the rest of us weren't smiling with him. "I don't mean it like that. I'm only sayin' it's a perfect opportunity to make a presence. To make a name for ourselves outside the Celts. I've only made acquaintances with a few of the Greeks, but believe me when I say that lot knows how to get in trouble. And if Zeus is asking for our help, they *need* it."

Phoebe moved to the center between us. "I've always wanted to visit Greece. Can we tag along? We can look around while you two handle your business on Olympus."

"Olympus?" I breathed out, my hand moving to my open mouth. "Do you really think that's where they want to meet us?"

Erimon shrugged. "As far as I know, most of them don't live in Greece any longer, so I can't imagine they'd mean anywhere else."

And here I thought I'd gotten a handle on all things magical and mythical. All it took was the idea of stepping foot on Mount Olympus to throw me for another ethereal reel.

"What about Finn or Mave or—" I folded my arms over my stomach.

Erimon chuckled and cupped my elbows. "They're all off on other missions. This one is for us to handle. The Greeks aren't asking us to show up and fight a minotaur straight away or anything."

"What do you say, Eira? After you finish your royal business you can tour Greece with me and Patrick. Just like old times." Phoebe's eyes glistened with hope and joy.

Patrick kissed her cheek. "Just like old times."

Emrys flew to my shoulder and nuzzled my chin, as if it

were the final action I needed to feel secure.

"Let's schedule a meeting then," I announced.

Phoebe clapped her hands together, and Patrick lifted her from the floor, twirling them.

"To Greece," Phoebe shouted.

Erimon strode to where our crowns lay, picking both up and strolling back to me. He slid mine atop my head, pinching my chin with his thumb and forefinger and kissing me tenderly. "I go where you go, my queen."

Setting Erimon's crown on his head, losing myself in those sparkling cerulean eyes, I wrapped my hands around his neck and beamed at him. "Because *that* is the power of eternity."

THE END

Balor – (bail-er)

Bandruí - (ban-dree)

Eira - (ay-rah)

Emrys – (em-riss)

Erimon - (ehre-mahn)

Clíodhna – (clEE-nah)

Cu Chulainn - (Coo Cullen)

The Dullahan (Crom Dubh) - (doo-luh-han)

Finn MacCoul - (fin mək-KOOL)

Ilmarinen - (ilmα-rinen)

Mave (also spelled Maeve) – (mayv)

Morrigan – (mor-REE-gun)

Rhiannon – (ree-an-non)

Carly Spade's *The Druid Duo* is complete:

Power of Eternity (Book 1)
Eternally Yours (Book 2)

Catch the first book in the Contemporary Mythos series:

HADES

The King of the Underworld may have found a woman
truly capable of melting his cold, dark heart.

HADES (Contemporary Mythos, #1)
BUY IT ON AMAZON

ACKNOWLEDGEMENTS

First and foremost, I'd like to ultimately thank THE READERS. I know some of you have been waiting for this story since Power of Eternity (my FIRST published book) released in 2019 and I can't express my gratitude enough for your patience. I do truly think (and hope) this was worth the wait because of how far I've come not only as a writer but a story teller. This book has become something far more involved than I'd originally anticipated and I'm ecstatic for it!

To my critique partner AK, you've also been with me since the initial creation of my warrior Druid and it's amazing being able to share this moment with you to say, it's FINALLY complete. We've both developed our strengths so much since we initially first started talking and I think the Druid Duo itself speaks that in volumes.

To Cerys, your excitement as my alpha reader continues to breathe new life into my lungs and I always look forward to our fun and honest chats as you read each chapter. So glad that you got to fall in love with Erimon as much as I have.

To my husband, thank you for not batting an eyelash at the whirlwind our house has become these last couple weeks as I've been determined to get edits done and that meant the upkeep kind of, sort of took a backburner (or it just plain did). You're my rock and always have been.

Again, to all my loyal readers and new, I truly hope you enjoy this Celtic fantasy world I created and though the Druids own story has come to a close, you'll definitely see them pop up elsewhere in the future.

Sláinte!

STAY TUNED!

WWW.CARLYSPADE.COM